Just Like Jenny

Sandy Asher grew up in Philadelphia where she was always busy acting, dancing and writing. She attended Indiana University, and now lives in Missouri with her husband and two children, where she is special instructor in creative writing at Drury College, Springfield.

Mrs Asher has had many short stories, poems and plays published in America, as well as four novels for young readers. *Just Like Jenny* is her second novel to be published in Fontana Lions; the first was *Friends and Sisters*.

Sandy Asher

Just Like Jenny

Lions

First published in Great Britain 1982 by Victor Gollancz Ltd
First published in Lions 1984
8 Grafton Street, London W1X 3LA
Fourth impression August 1987

Lions is an imprint of
the Children's Division, part of
the Collins Publishing Group

Copyright © 1982 by Sandy Asher

Printed in Great Britain by
William Collins Sons & Co. Ltd, Glasgow

For Emily

1

"Ehh-vvv-ery-body out!"

Mr. Oldham's voice boomed from the studio, setting off a stampede of black leotards and pink tights toward the dressing room door.

"Hurry up, Steph!" Jenny called back over her shoulder.

"I can't find my waistband," I said, frantically flapping a towel with one hand and my empty dance bag with the other.

"What?" Jenny turned in the doorway.

"My waistband, I can't find it. I must have left it home."

Mr. Oldham has this rule: We have to wear white elastic waistbands so we can check our hip alignment in the mirror. Mr. Oldham has a lot of rules, and if you break one, he can make you feel one step lower than a slug squished under a rock.

Jenny dumped the contents of her dance bag onto the floor and rummaged through the towels and extra tights.

"Oh, God, I don't have another one with me. Well,

come on, everybody's at the barre. We're going to be late. Maybe he won't notice," she offered.

"Late" is right up there with "unprepared" among the things you never want to be in front of Mr. Oldham. It's not that he murders you or anything; it's more that he makes you wish you were dead.

"Fat chance he won't notice," I said. I slammed my dance bag shut and hurried out after Jenny, who had her waistband on. So did every single other girl in the class. Five whole weeks to forget in and no one forgot. Except me.

Mr. Oldham noticed. He notices everything. I guess that's why he's the best dancing teacher in Hartford, and probably all of Connecticut. (He used to be one of the best dancers in the whole country, until he hurt his back in a car wreck.) Anyway, he didn't say anything; he just stood across the room from me and glared at the place where my waistband should have been. He glared for a long time, long enough for every girl in the room, plus that creepy little pianist of his, to turn and look at me while my ears burned and my palm soaked the barre with sweat. Satisfied at last with my humiliation, Mr. Oldham strode to the front of the studio.

I took a couple of deep breaths, found a dry spot on the barre for my hand, tucked in my tummy and my derriere and made a silent vow to *show him*. I'd outdance everybody; boy, would I ever. I'd dance so well, I'd reduce him to tears. He'd be on his knees begging my forgiveness, offering me a lifetime supply of waistbands if only I'd agree to be *prima ballerina* of the Oldham Dance Workshop, the performing troupe made up of his very best dancers. I'd tell him I'd have to think it over; I had other offers to consider.

Seriously, in the five weeks Mr. Oldham had been gone choreographing musical comedies for a summer stock company up in the Berkshire Mountains, I'd practiced hours every day. I'd even managed to perfect a double pirouette, on pointe, to the left, my weaker side. I couldn't wait to show him how much I'd improved. I was sure he'd be impressed. I'd imagined his pleased smile over and over again while I'd stretched and spun in my basement practice room. Pleasing Mr. Oldham has always been more important to me than getting all A's in school—and it's a lot harder. But pleasing him right now was more important than ever. Just before leaving for the Berkshires he'd warned us: "This coming year will be the turning point for this class. Some of you will give up dancing in favor of proms and cheerleading and such stuff as ordinary mortals find important. Some of you will opt for safety and remain good amateurs for life. And one or two or three of you—the gifted, gutsy few—will begin your breakthrough to the world of professional dance. This coming year, *I'll know.*"

Several people had quit, just as he'd predicted. Dear God, I prayed, let me be one of the gifted, gutsy few. Let me show him the best class of my life.

What I showed him instead was the worst. The harder I tried, the clumsier I got; the clumsier I got, the harder I tried. I was trapped in a world war: feet against the ankles, floor against the feet, knees against each other, and everybody against the brain. By the time we got to the petits battements, Mr. Oldham decided to inspect the battlefield more closely.

"Front, side, back, side, back, side, front, side," he barked, standing right behind me and snapping his fingers to the beat. But he and that weasel of a pianist seemed to be racing me to the finish—and winning. Instead of a series of precise little kicks, my petits battements were more like a severe nervous twitch. When the exercise finally ended, I caught a glimpse of Mr. Oldham in the mirror across the front wall. He was shaking his head in dismay.

When my turn came to cross the floor alone, doing chaîné turns and grands jetés and all that, I twisted my ankle the first time around and ended up hanging over the barre near the big French windows, gasping for air while everyone else whizzed by.

Then came the adagio. I was so frazzled I couldn't keep my balance for a split second, let alone the required number of counts. Rather than topple the rest of my group like a row of pink and black dominoes, I gave up and slouched to the back of the room. The pianist sneered at me as I passed.

"Nordland!" Mr. Oldham bellowed. "We are not here to admire the view. Please repeat the adagio with the next group." He ran both hands through his longish salt-and-pepper hair, throwing his head back as if I were causing him to lose his mind. Mr. Oldham can be very dramatic. His voice booms as if he were constantly addressing someone on the last row of the second balcony of a theater. "And stay

4

to the rear, if you will, Nordland," he went on. "I'm just giving you a second chance out of the goodness of my heart."

The class tittered. Jenny rolled her eyes heavenward in sympathy. My throat went bone dry. Flushed as I was from exertion, I could feel my cheeks going beyond red as I crept into the back line of the second group. I'd already forgotten the combination, of course. Despair can do that to you. The most I could hope for was to catch a hint of each step from the girls in front of me. The trick was to copy it without looking as if I were copying.

"On second thought," Mr. Oldham said, enunciating each word as if it were coated in lemon, "since you've already had one stab at it—nearly fatal—why don't you come up front here and lead us? It occurs to me that you require close observation this evening."

In utter misery I shuffled up to the front row. The pianist began his maudlin dirge. For a mad moment I had a terrific urge to slam the piano shut on his fingers, laugh like a maniac, and dive through the open windows to the pavement two stories below.

But I didn't jump. I danced. Sort of. With the help of the others' reflections in the mirror and some harsh corrections from Mr. Oldham, I muddled through.

At last the first hour ended and I dragged myself toward the dressing room to get my toe shoes.

"Just one minute, Nordland."

It was Mr. Oldham, his hands firmly planted on my slumped shoulders, his huge voice vibrating in my brain. He spun me around to face him, while Jenny and the others stood clumped by the dressing room door, watching.

"I don't know what you've been doing these past five weeks, Nordland," Mr. Oldham said, "but it's obvious dancing wasn't high on your list. You are capable of much better work than you've shown tonight. At least I used to think you were. I've never been wrong before, but there's always a first time, isn't there?"

If it were possible to die of shame, I would have been a goner. I couldn't tell Mr. Oldham how much I'd practiced. First of all, he wouldn't have believed me. And second, to practice all those hours and still be so bad really made me a lost cause. Mr. Oldham swung me around again so that I was facing the dressing room. Mercifully, the other girls had disappeared inside.

"Go forth," he commanded, "and be prepared to work. Or be prepared to forget it, Nordland. I don't allow people to waste my time."

Somehow I reached the safety of the dressing room, where Jenny draped a damp arm around me and gave me an encouraging squeeze. "Hang in there, Steph," she said. The other girls muttered in agreement, but they avoided looking directly at me, as if my failure were an embarrassment to them all.

"He sneered at me," I murmured, furiously blinking back tears.

"Who did?" Jenny wanted to know.

"That pimply creep of a pianist."

"Wilbur the Weasel? He sneers at everybody."

The room warmed with anger at Wilbur the Weasel. Complaining about Wilbur was our hobby. It got us through the times when we wanted to give up dancing forever or to murder Mr. Oldham in cold blood. Giving up dancing would be like mailing ourselves to hell. And how could you murder the man who was holding your ticket to heaven? So poor weird Wilbur took the blame for everything.

By the time we had our toe shoes on, we'd worked him over good, from his flaky, red scalp right down to the chewed-up rubber on his filthy sneakers. I felt a lot better then, shaky still, but ready to give it another try. After all, that double pirouette on pointe to the left was coming right up, wasn't it?

It wasn't. In minutes I collapsed against the barre again, the soft evening breeze rippling little chills along my sweaty body and tears blurring my eyes. Instead of doing a double pirouette on pointe to the left, I'd keeled over right under Mr. Oldham's nose. He'd stood there, between me and the mirror, arms folded, waiting for me to fail, expecting it, practically willing it. And I had. Only then did he move away, muttering something under his breath, I don't know what and it's probably just as well. Biting my lip to stop the tears, I turned around to watch the second group, Jenny among them. Or, rather, Jenny above and beyond them. She didn't just dance, she took off in flight. Her arms swooped and fluttered, her legs flashed and leaped and spun. Even her face danced; light danced in her eyes. Glissade, pas de bourrée, *balancé, balancé*, step right, to fourth position, and pir—ou—ette. There it was. My double pirouette on pointe to the left. Except I wasn't doing it. Jenny was. Perfectly.

When the music stopped and Jenny descended from her flight, she smiled up at Mr. Oldham and he smiled back. He actually smiled at her! Mr. Oldham never smiles. Well, practically never. Maybe once every fifty-seven gallons of sweat and a hundred and ten pulled muscles. But he sure did smile at Jenny just then.

That's when it hit me, like a shower of ice raising steam from my overheated head: Jenny was going to make it. She was really going to be a dancer. Just as we'd both hoped and planned and dreamed about for years.

And where did that leave me?

2

Jenny and I have been going to the Oldham Dance Academy for seven years. That's where we met, way back when I was six and she was eight. My mom has a photograph hanging in our dining room of Jenny and me in our first recital that spring. We look like two little fat-cheeked dolls in huge ruffly pink bonnets. Jenny is smiling brightly at the camera and pointing her toe out in front of her. I'm standing beside her, kind of knock-kneed, as if I have to go to the bathroom, and I'm looking at her foot with this confused expression on my face, as if to say, "What are you doing that for, Jenny? Are you stepping on a bug?"

We've danced in four recitals since then, one every other year. But I can still remember the excitement of that first one, the hugeness of the auditorium and the shock of seeing Mr. Oldham in a tuxedo instead of the black slacks and T-shirt he always teaches in. I think that was the first time I felt a little bit afraid of him—and a little bit in love with him. Not that he was strict with us when we were beginners. Oh, no.

In fact, I remember our giggling in those days more than I remember our dancing. It's when he has you hooked, when he knows you'd rather dance than eat, that he turns into an ogre.

And Jenny and I sure are hooked on dancing. Three times a week, we ride that Farmington Avenue bus together from West Hartford into the city. On Tuesdays and Thursdays we take ballet from six thirty to seven thirty and toe from seven thirty to eight. On Saturdays we take a class from ten thirty to noon that combines modern dance and jazz techniques.

I've always admired Jenny and tried to be like her, right from that first day when she bounced into the studio with her long black hair swinging below her waist. Every night for years I tugged each hair on my head, trying to make it grow faster and straighter and longer. But it never did. Mom says that when I was little, I'd sometimes talk to myself in the mirror and call my reflection Jenny. I don't remember that at all, and it sounds pretty weird to me, but Mom says it's not unusual for an only child to do that.

I've always liked Jenny being older and better at things than me. It gave me something to shoot for. I'll get there, I'd tell myself; someday, I'll be just like Jenny. I can remember when we were small, I thought Jenny was some kind of magician because she was always cleaner and neater than I was. I thought it was a trick, a magical spell that she knew and I didn't. That beautiful hair of hers practically squeaks with cleanliness and even when we used to turn somersaults on the green shag carpet in my living room, it would float back into place instantly. My light brown fuzz would snap and crackle with electricity and stand out stiff to its frazzled ends like something gruesome from outer space.

I used to think that when I got to be Jenny's age, nine or ten or eleven or whatever was right up the road there, I'd catch up to her in every way. But each birthday, she'd still be two years and thirty-three days ahead of me, and able to do something new that I couldn't quite manage yet. Like scoop up all ten jacks one-handed on a single bounce of the ball. Or polish her right-hand nails left-handed and *neatly*—and then not pick off all the polish within an hour. Or turn double pirouettes on pointe to the left.

"You looked terrific out there, Jen," I told her in the dressing room after class, desperate to keep up a brave front despite everything. I peeled off the back of her leotard for her, then continued tugging off my soggy tights. "Really terrific."

"Thanks, Stephie." She was fussing with her towel, delicately patting her face and neck dry. I knew she was feeling bad for me and I wished she wouldn't. It made me feel doubly rotten, once for the way I'd danced and once for being an embarrassment to her.

The other girls from our class and some new ones from the Oldham Workshop wiggled and wedged themselves between us on their way from hooks to benches to mirrors, so we couldn't talk for a while. I sank onto a bench and pulled on my jeans, a wave of exhaustion washing over me from the throbbing new blisters on my toes to the roots of my disheveled hair.

When Jenny finished dressing, she came over and sat beside me. The dressing room had emptied by then. I was tying my sneakers and taking a long time with them.

"Stephie, don't worry about tonight," she said. "Everybody has an off night now and then."

Kind as her words were, I didn't want to hear them. What I wanted was a miracle that would make her forget what she'd seen, a magic wand to wipe my humiliation out of her memory forever.

I yanked a lace so hard it snapped in two. "Nuts," I said, and threw the dirty bit of shoelace across the room. "I practiced so hard."

"I know you did. And it'll show next time."

"You think so?"

"Sure."

How could she be so sure? *I* was sure I'd do well after all those hours of practicing and I was awful. I'd practiced and I'd tried with everything in me and nothing had gone right. That really scared me. I didn't mention it to Jenny. How could I? Nothing scared Jenny. Not Mr. Oldham, not tests in school, not boys, nothing. So I kept my fear to myself, knotted my broken lace together, and gathered the rest of my stuff in silence.

The Oldham Workshop dancers were warming up when Jenny and I left the dressing room. The Workshop is Mr. Oldham's semiprofessional dance troupe. That means sometimes they get paid and sometimes they don't, depending on where they perform. They rehearse almost every night of the week, plus Saturday afternoons. You have to give up a lot for that— most of your private life, in fact—but you get to perform all over New England. It's a big honor for Mr. Oldham to invite you to audition for the Workshop. Jenny and I have always said we'd gladly give up our *teeth* if he ever asked us.

No one is allowed to watch Workshop rehearsals. That's another of Mr. Oldham's rules. But Jenny devised this plan to get around it. First, we dawdle in the dressing room after class until everybody else is gone and the rehearsal has begun. Once Mr. Oldham gets busy with the rehearsal, we hang back in the doorway of the dressing room and watch. Sometimes we've watched for ten or fifteen minutes before he's snapped his fingers at us from across the room and pointed emphatically toward the stairs. By the time we cross from the dressing room to the stairs and go down v-e-r-y s-l-o-w-l-y, we get another three-to-four minute peek.

This time Mr. Oldham's back was toward us. He had a hold on one boy's leg and was helping him stretch it over his head in an arabesque. I wasn't in that great a mood for Workshop watching and was actually heading for the stairs when Jenny grabbed me by the arm and nodded toward the front of the studio.

There was Trisha Jones, both legs straight out sideways in a Chinese split, stretching her body so that her chest was nearly to the floor *and* talking to another girl and *still* not taking her eyes off her own reflection in the mirror. I had to smile in spite of my foul mood. That Trisha! She needs a mirror like the rest of us need air. Jenny and I noticed it the very first time we saw her in Workshop. Mr. Oldham was lecturing to the group about something or other and everyone was seated at his feet, giving him their rapt attention. And there was Trisha, her eyes practically rolling off the side of her face, checking her profile in the mirror, first to the right, then the left, then with a little tilt thisaway and thataway, her long red ponytail bobbing right along. Finally Mr. Oldham noticed her and stopped talking. He stared straight down through the top of her skull, but she tried two or three more poses before she realized he—and everyone else—was looking at her. I've never seen anyone blush so brightly in my life. But did it cure her? It did not. No matter where she is in the dressing room or the studio, she's looking in the mirror: rear view, checking out the seams; side view, checking out the tummy; front view, checking out the entire divine shrine. It never seems fair to me that a conceited jerk like Trisha should be able to dance like an angel. But Trisha does.

Not that she looked like an angel just then. More like a Gila monster, actually. She'd touched her nose to the floor, then swiveled her eyeballs upward to catch the effect in the you-know-what. The strain made her face go all blotchy. I looked at Jenny and we both started giggling. Mr. Oldham turned just then and glowered in our direction from beneath his bushy white brows. We catapulted down the stairs and burst onto the street, roaring with laughter. Above our heads the Weasel's piano began to pulse its beat into the mild autumn air.

For the moment, laughing with Jenny all the way to the bus stop, I almost forgot what a failure I'd been.

3

I've always thought Mr. Oldham should get together with Mrs. Estelle Deveraux, the music teacher at my junior high. She's the only person I know who is even more dramatic than he is. Daddy says she's beyond dramatic; he calls her flamboyant.

Mrs. Deveraux wears her hair in a huge Afro, even though she's not black. In fact, her Afro is blond! And she wears these flowing, flowery tent-like dresses with a hundred gold chains around her neck and boots with such high heels they look like stilts. They make *her* look gigantic.

Her nails always match her outfits. And she wears tons of makeup and false eyelashes. Some kids say that's not all that's false. They think nobody's shaped like that naturally, not even Dolly Parton. I'm not so sure about that.

One thing I am sure of is that Mrs. Deveraux really is a good teacher, even if she does resemble an enormous flowering shrub. The boys giggle and gawk at her a lot, but I think that's because they like her more than they want to let on. I like her a lot, particularly because she lets us sing popular songs mixed in with the boring stuff in our music books. She especially loves songs from Broadway musicals, which suits me just fine.

One day not long after the school year started, she made us all change our seats so the boys were on one side of the room and the girls on the other. We were learning "Anything You Can Do" from *Annie Get Your Gun.*

"Annie is stage right; Frank Butler, stage left," Mrs. Deveraux explained. "He knows she's a better shot than he is. And she knows he knows. But she also knows she'll lose him if she outshoots him in public. He was a second-rate shot with a first-rate ego."

The boys groaned and the girls cheered.

"What do you think Annie does?" Mrs. Deveraux asked. "Does she miss the shot on purpose—or not? If you've seen the show or the movie, don't give it away yet." She winked at me, then, because she knows I love musical comedies.

"She misses the shot," Henry Porter yelled.

Just as Mrs. Deveraux was about to say, "Right," Debbie Wickham shouted, "She hits him over the head with her gun!" And we all cracked up.

That really put us in the mood for the song. By the third time through the chorus we were practically standing on our chairs. Even after the song ended, the boys went on yelling, "No, you can't!" while the girls screamed, "Yes, I can!"

Suddenly Mrs. Deveraux waved her hands over her head to stop us. "I have a wonnn-der-ful eye-dee-yah," she said. Every once in a while she talks like that, enunciating up a storm. She rippled the piano keys for added emphasis. "How would you like to show what you *really* can do? How about putting on a tahhhhh-lent show?"

We all looked at each other and kind of blinked in surprise.

"A real show, in the evening," Mrs. Deveraux went on. "I know you play instruments and sing and take all kinds of lessons. Wouldn't you like to show off a little?"

There were more blinks, with shrugs and a few shy snickers tossed in.

"Come, come, Steph-ah-nie, you could dance for us, could you not?" Mrs. Deveraux likes to say "could you not" and "is it not" and "do we not" from time to time.

"I . . . uh . . . guess so," I said, not really expecting her to go through with it. She's quite a dreamer. Last year, in seventh grade, she told Henry Porter she could see him at Carnegie Hall, roses pelting the stage after one of his pee-*yah*-no con-*cher*-tohs. Henry'd only been playing the pee-*yah*-no for about three weeks.

"There you have it," Mrs. Deveraux cried, on her feet now, beaming at me and sweeping her arm over the class in a dramatic arc. "Act One, Scene One: Steph-ah-nie Norrrd-lahnd, Prrreeema Ballerrreeeeena! Henry, you do have a con-*cher*-toh ready by now, do you not?"

Henry Porter snorted and Timothy Brown, behind

him, gave him a friendly whack on the head. "I—
um—uh—*ow*! Quit it, Brown. I can almost play 'Für
Elise,' Mrs. Deveraux. My teacher is making me
memorize it."

"Wonderful! Who else, now? Speak up. It is wrong
to be shy about your *tah*-lents, is it not?"

By the end of the period we had one tap dancer,
three pianists, two guitar players, a magic act, and
me, Steph-ah-nie Norrrrd-lahnd, Prrrreeeeema Bah-
lerrreeeena!

In the next day or two so many other seventh and
eight grades volunteered that the show promised to
be five hours long. Our principal, Mr. Langley, suggested we charge admission and buy new books for
the library with the proceeds. Mrs. Deveraux was in
seventh heaven. She immediately rigged up a "call-
board" outside the cafeteria with all our names and
the first rehearsal posted on it. It also had a sign in
big black letters on red construction paper: FIRST
ANNUAL ALL-SCHOOL TALENT SHOW, THURSDAY, DECEMBER
13, 8:15 P.M.

4

"I think it's a terrific idea," Mom said, when she got home from work and I told her about the talent show. I followed her into her bedroom to fill in the details while she changed out of her dress and into slacks. "Have you started working on a dance?" she asked, unscrewing a loopy gold earring.

"No, not yet," I admitted.

"No time like the present," Mom said.

That's Mom for you. If there's a job to be done, she does it. *Now*. No ifs, ands, or buts about it. She and a friend of hers own this clothing boutique and Mom runs the store just like she runs our house: perfectly. "A place for everything and everything in its place" is another of her mottoes.

Daddy never thought she could run both a business and a home like that, but she showed him.

"I don't understand why you even *want* to work," he told her that fateful evening when she broke the news about opening a boutique. She'd just served dessert. Chocolate pudding. I'll never forget it.

"I'm already working," she said. "I clean and cook and wash and iron and chauffeur and shop and—"

"That's another thing," Daddy said. "Who's going to do all those things around here if you're out working?"

Mom swallowed a spoonful of pudding and looked Daddy straight in the eye. "Oink, oink," she said, to let him know he was being a male chauvinist pig.

"Now, wait just a minute here," Daddy said. "I think women ought to be allowed to work. I think they ought to receive equal pay. But when I come home from a long day at the office, I want a hot dinner on the table, by golly."

"Oh, *oink!*" Mom said, dropping her spoon back into the bowl in disgust.

"Will you stop oinking at me?" Daddy squealed. I was trying so hard not to laugh, I almost choked on a mouthful of milk. But it's true, Daddy's always insisting on a "hot dinner on the table, by golly," or "a pressed shirt in the closet, by golly," or "clean shorts in that drawer, by golly." Not that Mom doesn't always have them there. She does. But Daddy likes to point out how important such things are in the life of a hardworking businessman.

He's not mean, though. In fact, he's really kind of softhearted. He buys Mom flowers sometimes just for a "Happy Tuesday." Once he bought her the most delicious chocolate-covered almonds. The card read, "Ellie, Happy October 11, seven forty-three P.M., seventeenth anniversary of our first kiss. Love, Sam."

He gave them to her right in the middle of *The Muppet Show*. Mom cried. I got sick from eating too many chocolate-covered almonds. (Normally, I never eat candy, because there is nothing more pathetic than a fat dancer. But every once in a while, I go berserk. From sugar deprivation, I guess.)

Daddy is district sales manager for a novelty gift company, so I guess he's just naturally big on gifts. We have ashtrays and mugs all over the house that say things like "Aloha from Hawaii" and "Howdy from Dallas." Daddy gets free samples. He agrees that most of his products are dumb-looking and silly, but "A job is a job," he says. "And it puts bread on the table, by golly."

Anyway, Mom poked at her pudding with her spoon once or twice, then plowed right ahead: "Sam, I want to get out of the house and be with people. I'm bored here by myself all day. And I couldn't get the house any cleaner if I poured boiling water over the whole thing and sterilized it. One of my friends from the C-R group—"

"Oh, no, not that again," Daddy cried. "I should have guessed that had something to do with it. You and that damned feminist gang of yours, that conscious or unconscious or whatever it is . . ."

"Consciousness-raising. It's a consciousness-raising group. It helps women become aware of their potential."

"Yeah, well, if you raise your consciousness any higher, it's going to go into orbit."

"Oh, Sam, listen to me," Mom pleaded.

Daddy heaved a giant sigh. "I'm listening," he said. I could tell he was weakening. A few more minutes and Mom would have him.

"This friend, Frieda Myers, has a wonderful idea for a shop, a small but very elegant boutique. I just know it'll work and I know I can help her make it work. And eventually, I'll be able to put away some money for Stephie's college expenses."

"Can't her husband pay for that?"

"Daddy!"

Mom had a lot more arguments in favor of the shop than Daddy could muster against it, so she got her way. She always does. He didn't like her cutting her hair later, either, not at first. "I don't need a wife who looks just like me!" he said. And she kind of *does*, now, since they're both slender, with short sandy hair and blue eyes. But somehow she convinced him that short hair was more convenient *and* more becoming. She's a very determined person. Determined and organized—there's no way you can beat a combination like that. It's not that she's a germicidal maniac like Timothy Brown's mom, who makes him carry this little folding toothbrush kit to school and brush after every meal and snack. It's just that Mom can walk across a messy room and have it straightened up by the time she gets to the other side. So it's not surprising that she can run a store, polish the house, and have a hot meal on the table when Daddy gets home from work, by golly. Or that she expects me to have a dance choreographed three hours after Mrs. Deveraux announces a talent show.

Daddy's reaction to the talent show was different from Mom's. He stabbed his fork into his pot pie, pulled out a chunk of chicken, and said, "That Deveraux woman is going to organize a show? I don't believe it. Has she organized her hair yet?"

Mom dabbed at her mouth with a napkin. "Sam," she said, "you really shouldn't say things like that about Stephie's teachers. Besides, I like Mrs. Deveraux. She's got flair."

"You mean she *looks* like a flare," Daddy said. "And acts like one, too."

"You know what?" Mom said, folding her napkin neatly and placing it beside her plate. "I don't remember the names of a single one of my staid, dignified teachers. But I do remember Mr. Hogarth. He read us poetry with such passion he once stepped into the wastepaper basket beside his desk, fell over backward, and cracked his elbow. His arm was in a cast for weeks."

"Sounds like a fool," Daddy said.

"Your problem," Mom informed him, "is that you've never understood people who truly *love* their work."

"What's that supposed to mean?" Daddy asked her.

"I rest my case," Mom said.

Dad grunted and shoveled in the last of his pie crust.

(I never eat pie crust. Or potatoes. Or the coating on fried chicken. Well, almost never. Sometimes on Saturdays after dancing class Jenny and I are so exhausted and so hungry, we simply cannot make it past the McDonald's between us and the bus stop. So we go in and gorge ourselves on two or three large orders of fries apiece and milkshakes. But I never eat that stuff at home. It drives Mom crazy.)

"Stephanie, eat your pie crust," she said, as she always does.

"I can't, Mom. It's fattening."

"Stephanie, I put a lot of time and effort into making that crust from scratch."

"I know. And I'm sure it's delicious. But I have to watch my weight."

"Your weight?" Daddy put in. "What weight are you watching? You're all skin and bones. What weight are you talking about?"

"A dancer has to be thin, Daddy," I reminded him.

"Oh, of course," he said, with a mocking little nod. "A dancer has to be thin. How could I have forgotten?"

"Sam," Mom started to interrupt. But Daddy was off and running.

"First of all," he announced, "you're not a dancer yet. You're a little girl. And second of all, you look like a skeleton waiting for Halloween. And third of all, you are wasting food, which means you are wasting my hard-earned *money*. Now, eat . . . your . . . pie crust." The last three words were accompanied by a finger poked in the direction of the calories in question.

"Daddy, I can't."

"You can and you will. Now, *do*."

There was nothing left for me but to pull a Jenny on them. I nibbled at the crust ever so slowly until Daddy got up and went into the living room to get himself comfortable for the evening news and Mom got busy loading all the dishes except mine into the dishwasher. Then I waited an appropriate moment or two, gathered up my plate and glass, and headed for the disposal. In a flash the pie crust was gone and my nicely rinsed plate was in the washer.

"Thank you, dear," Mom said.

"My pleasure," I assured her. Then I moved on to more serious matters. "Do you think Mr. Oldham would help me choreograph a dance for the talent show?"

"He should," Daddy yelled in from the living room. "We've paid him enough over the years."

"Oh, Sam, hush," Mom told him, calling back over her shoulder as she maneuvered the milk and salad dressing into the packed refrigerator. "I think you ought to choreograph something yourself," she said, flipping the door shut triumphantly.

"I couldn't make up a whole dance."

"Have you ever tried?"

Ever since that C-R group started meeting, Mom thinks there's nothing in the world women can't do if they try. Before that, she knew there was nothing *she* couldn't do if she tried. It was the rest of womankind, including me, she only recently became sure about.

"Well, Jenny and I mess around a little. We make up dances to our records, you know, stuff like that."

"There you go. After you finish your homework, go downstairs and 'mess around a little.' "

"All by myself? Without Jenny?"

"Sure. Why not?"

I shrugged because I couldn't think of an answer. But it just didn't seem right somehow.

The first thing I did, though, even before homework, was call Jenny and tell her about the talent show.

"Oh, Steph, that's wonderful!" she cried. "What's the date? I'll put it down on my calendar right now so I won't forget."

"December thirteenth. It's a Thursday. I guess I'll have to miss class."

"Mr. Oldham won't mind. Not if you're performing, especially a solo. Oh, Steph, I'm so excited for you."

"Yeah, well, I have to make up a dance, I guess."

"Sure. Let me know if you need any help. Oh, I can't wait to see you up there all by yourself. You'll be great. I just know it."

Buoyed by Jenny's confidence in me, I went downstairs to my practice room ready to work. Actually it's a recreation room, but Daddy set up a barre and mirrors for me ages ago. He grumbled a lot, but Mom insisted that if I was going to take classes, I needed to practice, and if I was going to practice, I needed proper equipment. "If it's worth doing, it's worth doing right," she said. "Who decided it was worth doing?" Daddy muttered. "I don't remember voting." But after a false start or two he finally got it done.

"Waste of time and money," he assured me, as I ventured in to test out my new equipment for the very first time. But he did give me a little pat on the derriere, so I figured he only half meant what he'd said.

I warmed up and stretched till I ached, then stretched a little more for good measure. One thing about dancing: You get used to pain. Aching muscles actually start to feel *good* because you know you're using them. When I felt really warmed up, I started flipping through my albums on the record rack under the stereo. I wanted something kind of upbeat. I knew Mrs. Deveraux was thinking more in terms of ballet, but I couldn't picture myself doing that at school. Some kids think ballet is corny. They're wrong, of course, but they think it just the same. It's not surprising, I guess, when some adults think it's corny, too. Like Daddy. "What's the point?" he once asked me after a recital. "What do you want to flip and flutter around like that for? Half of it looks silly and the other half looks downright painful."

But even Daddy enjoys the modern jazz routines in musical comedies. "Now, that's got a little pep to it" is the way he puts it. I almost hate to admit it, because I know ballet is the most demanding and most beautiful of all dancing, but I really kind of like modern jazz best myself. So the ideal choice, it seemed to me, would be a modern jazz number to something from a Broadway show. Something with a little pep to it.

I have quite a collection of original cast albums. I

spend hours in the basement, singing and dancing along, imagining what the shows might look like—with me in all the starring roles, of course.

I finally settled on "Something's Coming" from *West Side Story*. I put on the record, stood up, swayed back and forth a few times, and waited for inspiration to strike me. It didn't. I shuffled my feet around a little, but I felt so awkward. And silly. Every step I tried, I got a queasy feeling that everyone'd laugh and I'd feel like such a fool. I could just picture them all leaving the auditorium, eyes rolling, and muttering under their breath like Daddy.

I needed Jenny there. I felt lost without her. Empty. And empty-headed. The first rehearsal was less than two weeks away. I wondered how many of our routines we were supposed to have ready by then. Henry Porter already had "Für Elise" almost memorized. What was I going to do for *my* act? Put on a record and sway?

5

What a mob of kids showed up for the first talent show rehearsal! Even Mrs. Deveraux looked overwhelmed as she trotted onto the stage and surveyed the masses gathered before her. Twisting and squirming in my front-row aisle seat, I counted thirty-four kids before Mrs. Deveraux started talking and I had to face front.

Barbara Crane was sitting beside me. She's a nice kid and my best school friend, but she's not my best friend in the whole world, like Jenny. Barbara wants to be in show business, too, but she wants to sing.

"How are so many people going to be in one show?" she was whispering while her fingers wandered nervously over her chin, visiting from pimple to pimple. Barbara has very sensitive skin. In fact, she's sensitive inside and out—everything makes her nervous, so everything gives her pimples. "You think we'll have to audition?" she wondered aloud. "Do you think some kids won't make it?"

That idea set *my* stomach to quivering. How could

I audition? I still didn't have a dance choreographed. All Barbara had to do was sing her favorite Streisand song. She has every one of them memorized. But I couldn't get up there and imitate Margot Fonteyn!

How were so many people going to squeeze into one show?

"Ladies and gentlemen," Mrs. Deveraux began. "I want to welcome each and every one of you to the First Annn-yu-well—I hope—All-School Tahhhh-lent Show.

"Actually, this will not be a rehearsal in the true sense of the word. All I want you to do today is to fill out one of these forms." She stooped over to pick up a pile of forms at the edge of the stage. There was some odd coughing from a couple of boys right behind me, a kind of strangled hysteria. Mrs. Deveraux bending over has that effect on boys, especially jerks.

"Steph-ah-nie, you'll pass these forms around for me, will you not?"

I stood up and took them from her. Her long, curved nails were orange today, I noticed, orange to match the rust tones of her newest flowered dress. Her lipstick, rouge, and eye shadow were also in the orange to brown range. I don't know what perfume she was wearing, but I wouldn't be surprised if it was called Orange Blossom. I'll have to tell Daddy, I thought, that in her way, Mrs. Deveraux is actually quite organized.

I tried giving the forms out one at a time, but my hands were trembling, so I just held out the pile and let each person in an aisle seat peel a few off. Besides the kids from my class, there were a bunch of seventh graders, all huddled together and cackling like a flock of nervous chickens, and a few kids like Matt Greenspan and Anita Coopersmith from the other eighth grades. I knew them, but not very well. At our school, classes pretty much stick together. But Matt said "hi" as he took his forms off the pile. He's kind of cute, actually. He plays basketball and can usually be seen carrying one around under his arm. Just staying prepared, I guess, in case a game suddenly flares up between classes.

I returned the extra forms to Mrs. Deveraux and sat down.

"Did you take one for yourself?" she asked, waving a form in my direction.

"Oh, no. I forgot."

Everyone laughed a lot harder than I thought necessary. I grabbed the form and sat down again, fast. One of the fools behind me kicked my seat and gurgled maliciously. I wondered what his talent was. Probably slapping his flippers together and playing bicycle horns with his nose. Your typical eighth-grade boy.

The form asked for our name, home phone number, and our homeroom teacher's name. Then there was a space to describe what we intended to perform in the show. I wrote: "I plan to perform a modern jazz dance to the song 'Something's Coming' from the Broadway musical comedy *West Side Story.*"

Then you had to list your training and past performing experience. I put down: "I have studied seven years of ballet and two years of modern and jazz dancing at Oldham Academy in Hartford. We have a recital every other year. I've been in ballet numbers in four recitals and last year was also in a modern number and a jazz routine."

I didn't mention that Daddy nearly passed out last spring when he realized he'd have to pay for three costumes instead of one. But, in the end, I *think* he was proud of me. "I liked the routine with the high kicks," he admitted. And he and Mom sent me three long-stemmed yellow roses backstage.

After we'd passed our forms up to Mrs. Deveraux, she said, "As you may have noticed on the call-board, I asked you not to bring your instruments or music today. However, I do expect you to be prepared to perform at our next meeting, two weeks from today. That will be Wednesday, October 10 at 7:15 A.M."

Everyone groaned at that. Mrs. Deveraux pursed her lips for a moment, then continued: "I'm not expecting polished performances at that time. I just want to get some i-dee-yah of what you have planned. Please consult the call-board now and ah-gain for future announcements. There will be more frequent rehearsals as show time draws nearer. Thank you so much for coming this morning. It is eight twenty. You may go to your homerooms now."

Seats flapped, feet shuffled, and voices rose to a roar as the crowd filed out.

"Seven fifteen?" the weirdo behind me said. "I can't play the trumpet at seven fifteen. I can't even spit at seven fifteen."

"Yeah," his buddy agreed. "I don't know about this thing anyway. We've got football practice most mornings. I wouldn't have come at all, but my mother heard about it from my idiot sister and made me. I'm not playing that violin in front of anybody, not even a dog, and that's all there is to it."

Their shaggy blond heads bobbed up the aisle ahead of me.

"Good riddance," Barbara whispered. I agreed.

We soon understood why there hadn't been auditions. A lot more kids let it be known that they were dropping out as the idea sank in that there was going to be some *effort* involved, like getting up early and practicing.

"I think I'm going to sing 'People,' " Barbara announced at lunchtime. She'd spent the entire morning humming snatches of every Streisand song from "The Way We Were" to the entire score of *Funny Girl.*

"Yup. That's it. 'People.' I've made up my mind." With that, she piled her dishes on her tray and stood up. She'd been sitting across the table from me and I could see that her little heart-shaped face was set with determination under her strawberry-blond bangs. Her chin was held high and her eyes were squinted just a bit. That's her favorite Streisand pose, arrogant but noble. Barbara Crane is the only girl I know who wishes her nose were bigger.

I stood up, too, and gathered my things. "I'm glad one of us knows what she's doing," I said with a sigh.

But all was not lost. Fortunately, I'd already made plans to spend that Friday night at Jenny's house.

6

Jenny's house is a lot different from ours. First of all, it's more crowded. Jenny has two brothers and a sister: Pete Jr., who's ten; Ricky, eight; and Dawn, two. She also has a German Shepherd named Dog and a cocoa-colored part-Siamese named Cat. They spend most of their time growling and hissing and chasing each other all over the place. Jenny assures me they're just playing, but it looks a lot like attempted murder to me.

Then there are Jenny's parents. Her mom is really young-looking and she's pretty, like Jenny, with the same long, straight, thick black hair, only *hers* has a lot of silver in it. Mr. Gianino, on the other hand, is nearly bald. He's also about a foot shorter than Mrs. Gianino. Jenny takes after him in height. She and I are the same size and I'm the second shortest in my class. But Jenny's skinnier than me, sometimes by one pound, sometimes by five or six or even seven, depending on how insistent my parents have been about my eating.

Jenny's father calls us "petite." He's not petite, though. He's chubby. He looks like Pillsbury's Dough-boy, all round and pinchable and jolly. It's really kind of funny, because he does happen to be a baker. He even smells a little yeasty, like a warm loaf of bread fresh from the oven.

Mrs. Gianino is a free-lance commercial artist. She draws those newspaper ads for stores like my mom's boutique: ladies in fur coats and nightgowns and stuff like that. She has a drawing board set up in one cor-ner of her kitchen, but her drawings, newspaper clip-pings, brushes, pens, rulers, scissors, and who knows what else generally spill out everywhere.

"The minute Dawn starts first grade, I'm heading straight back to an office," she informed me as I ar-rived at the back door on Friday night. "Maybe then I'll be able to get this mess organized."

I picked my way carefully through the chaos on the kitchen floor, tightly clutching my duffle bag, record, dance bag, and jacket as I went.

"Unless you're pregnant by then," Mr. Gianino laughed. He was having a cup of coffee at the dining room table.

"Bite your tongue," Mrs. Gianino told him, but she laughed, too.

"Hi, Mr. Gianino," I called through the screen door that separated the kitchen from the rest of the house —and from the assorted children and animals.

"How-do, Stephanie."

Dog whined and scratched the bottom of the

screen to get my attention. Then Cat took a flying leap onto Dog's tail and off they charged into the living room and out of sight.

Mrs. Gianino shuffled some sketches and newspapers out of my way and unlatched the screen door. At the tiny sound of the hook falling, Dog and Cat raced back, each trying to be first into the kitchen.

"No! No!" Mrs. Gianino cried. "You've already had your dinner!"

Mr. Gianino slammed down his coffee cup, grabbed an animal's collar with each hand, and held them back while I scurried through the door with my gear and Mrs. Gianino locked herself in again.

Safe at last, Mrs. Gianino threw her head back and yelled, "Aaaaaaaaghhhh!" Mr. Gianino and I laughed and so did she, finally. He let the animals go. Immediately Cat popped Dog a few left jabs to the nose and they were off running again.

I love Jenny's house. It's crazy but fun. Mrs. Gianino says it's furnished in late-American Garage Sale. It's true that nothing matches anything else, but somehow it all fits together, the way a rainbow does.

"Where are the kids?" I asked.

"Worn out and bedded down," Mr. Gianino assured me.

I tiptoed up the stairs to Jenny's room. The door was closed, as usual. The door to Jenny's room is always closed. If it weren't, the room would be filled with animals and small children at all hours of the day and night. There's a big red STOP! sign taped to the outside of the door. Unfortunately, Dawn and the animals can't read.

"That you, Stephie?" Jenny called as I dropped my duffle bag trying to reach for the doorknob.

I opened the door and was struck, as always, by the difference between Jenny's room and mine. My room—like our whole house—has "antique-white" walls. Other than the windows, nothing stands between me and the purity of those walls but two framed prints of dancers and one oval mirror in a gilded frame. If Jenny's walls have a color, on the other hand, I've never seen it. From floor to ceiling, photographs clipped from *Dance* magazine jam against each other. They're not even framed. They're just glued right to the wall. Whenever Jenny feels like it, she glues a new one right on top of the old ones. About once a year I beg Mom to let me do my room the same way. She always gives the same response: "Over my dead body."

Jenny was lying on a blue mat in the middle of the bare wood floor, her legs thrown back over her head and her hips supported on her hands. The toothy grin embroidered on the back pocket of her jeans smiled at me upside down.

"Don't just stand there," she said. "Park it all somewhere and warm up. We're supposed to choreograph a dance tonight, aren't we?"

And we did. We put my record on the little phonograph in the corner of Jenny's room and began. By the time Mr. and Mrs. Gianino left for the movies, we were a third of the way through. Two and a half hours later when they came home and peeked in to say good night, we were finished. Jenny had had one great idea after another. About the only thing I'd contributed were those first few sways.

We were pretty worn out after that, so we got into our pajamas and climbed into bed. Jenny turned off the light.

"Are you going to use your real name?" she whispered in the dark. She didn't have to whisper. The Gianinos never make us be quiet and go to sleep the way my parents do. But something about the dark just makes it seem right to whisper.

"What do you mean?" I asked.

"For the talent show. Are you going to use your real name or your stage name? Stephanie Starr."

"Oh, come on," I said, giggling. "I never said that was my stage name."

"Yes, you did."

"When?"

"Don't you remember? It was Christmas vacation. I was in fifth grade, so you were in third. And Mom took us to New York to see Michael in *The Fantasticks*."

Michael is Jenny's cousin. He used to go to Oldham Academy and once, after a Workshop performance, he was asked to audition for the part of the Boy in *The Fantasticks*, an off-Broadway show, and he made it.

"Of course I remember that," I said. "How could I forget?"

"Well, Michael had changed his name from Gianino to Grant and you said you were going to change yours, too. To Stephanie Starr, with two r's. That's exactly what you said."

"I don't remember that," I said. "It sounds like a stripper."

We were chuckling over that when Jenny suddenly rolled over and flipped on the light.

"What's wrong?" I asked, blinking and shading my eyes.

"I forgot. I bought this week's *Variety*."

In a flash I was out of bed, too, peering over her shoulder at the newspaper in her hands.

"Lemme see!"

Jenny and I buy *Variety* whenever we can, which is whenever we're downtown and there happens to be one left on a newsstand. It's all about show business. It even lists auditions and what kind of people they're looking for, like: "FEMALE, FORTY-ISH, PUDGY, LOUD-MOUTHED." We keep hoping for someone to need a thirteen-ish or fifteen-ish petite, but so far nobody has.

"Look at this. They have a list of summer theaters," Jenny said, holding the paper out to me. Summer theaters have been a special dream of ours. We know we'll probably never get to be in a real professional show during a school year. But why not during the summer?

"Where?" I asked.

"Here, see? It's a rundown of how the summer theaters did financially. It also lists producers and locations. Connecticut has half a column."

Suddenly Jenny and I were looking at each other and reading each other's minds.

"Let's write them, Steph. Let's write to them about us."

I nodded. Immediately Jenny dug paper and pens out of her desk, and we jumped back into bed and spread the *Variety* out in front of us.

"What should we say?" I asked.

"Well, dear whoever, first of all." She peered down the column of names. "I'll start with this one, Mark Fitzsimmons at the Nutmeg. Here's the Music-Go-Round, Tom Hitchman. You do him."

I watched as Jenny wrote her return address and the date and "Dear Mr. Fitzsimmons" in her best handwriting, then started on mine.

"What next?" Jenny asked, pulling her pen back as if it might blotch her work.

It took a long time, but we finally composed a letter we both liked. It said:

> We are two young dancers, thirteen and fifteen years of age, who are extremely interested in professional careers. We study ballet, modern, and jazz dancing at the Oldham Academy, and we have appeared in four recitals. Could you please let us know if we could audition for your theater next summer? Thank you very much for your time and attention. We look forward to hearing from you soon.

The last two lines were what Jenny's mother always says in her business letters when she's writing to new clients. We thought they added a nice professional touch.

After we got the first two letters finished, we divided the rest of the names on the list and copied them over and over again. Finally, we addressed the envelopes, set them neatly on Jenny's bureau, and crawled back into bed. It was close to 2:00 A.M. and we were both bleary-eyed from writing.

"We'll mail them on the way to dancing school tomorrow," Jenny said, flipping the light off again.

"Okay. Do you think anyone will answer?"

"Maybe. You never know. It's worth a try. Maybe this could be the start for us. The start of something really big. Ladies and gentlemen, presenting Miss Stephanie Starr."

"Oh, good grief," I said, with a sigh. "Hey, did you make up a stage name, too, when I did?"

"Uh-huh."

"What was it?"

"Jennifer Jello."

At that I gave such a loud hoot that Dog, who sleeps outside Jenny's door, woofed. Jenny clapped a hand over my mouth.

"Shhhh! You'll wake everybody up."

Smothering our giggles in the pillows, we finally fell asleep.

7

"Stephie's going to be in a talent show at her school," Jenny announced, the minute she reached the top of the stairs and spotted Mr. Oldham at his desk. We were the first ones there. In spite of our late-night letter-writing campaign, we'd gotten up early and charged out of the house, eager to drop all our hopes into the corner mailbox. Then, already outside and all revved up, we'd caught an early bus.

I knew I'd have to tell Mr. Oldham about the talent show eventually, but I didn't expect Jenny to blurt it right out like that. I was more surprised than Mr. Oldham.

"Is that so?" he said, tilting his head to look me over as if he wasn't quite sure who I was. "What are you going to do, Nordland?"

"Dance," I said, suddenly feeling like a little kid answering the teacher's questions on her very first day of school.

Something like a nervous tic tugged at one corner of Mr. Oldham's mouth. He didn't make a sound, but

I was sure he was laughing at me. "I suspected that," he said. "What dance are you going to do?"

"We choreographed one last night," Jenny put in. "To 'Something's Coming' from *West Side Story*. Do you want to see it?"

"Oh, wait . . ." I began, but Mr. Oldham was already up and striding toward his record shelves.

"I've got a copy of that over here," he said. "Go change your clothes and warm up."

We did. You don't argue with Mr. Oldham. Jenny was all excited and bubbly. She didn't seem to notice that I was so nervous my toenails had turned purple. I clenched my feet to hide them from her. The only thing worse than being scared is letting Jenny know it.

Jenny did the dance with me. That helped. Watching the two of us bounce and whirl together in the long mirrors, I got to thinking we really didn't look too bad. I even managed a smile toward the end as I suddenly recalled Mr. Oldham's constant command: "When you dance, you *smile*. I don't want to know about your blisters. Smile!" Jenny, of course, beamed all the way through. Jenny always smiles when she dances, even when she is nervous, like at recitals. She says she doesn't have to think about it—dancing just makes her happy. It makes me happy, too, but I still have to remind myself to smile. And sometimes my lips tremble so much, I worry about them slithering right off my face.

When the music stopped, we both sank to the floor,

huffing and puffing. It was a lot harder dancing the routine full-out in the studio than it had been rehearsing it in bits and pieces in Jenny's room.

We looked at Mr. Oldham expectantly.

He gave us a thoughtful nod, then another, and a third.

"Okay," he said. Then he repeated it with one more nod for good measure. I was disappointed. Four nods and two okays weren't much to go on. Jenny and I scrambled to our feet and started toward the dressing room. Mr. Oldham was slipping the record back into its jacket.

"Nordland," he said.

"Yes?"

"Come here."

I walked over to him. He took his time replacing the record on the shelf and covering the record player while I just stood there. When he was perfectly satisfied with the record album's position and the safety and security of the record player, he turned and laid a heavy hand on each of my shoulders.

"You practice that dance," he said, his voice rumbling up from deep inside his chest, "until you can do it forward, backward, sideways, blindfolded, in your sleep, and in a heavy suit of armor. Understand?"

I nodded, trying hard to meet his steady slate-eyed gaze. I had to blink, though, because my eyes started watering.

"Good. No student of mine ever goes on a stage—any stage, anywhere, for any reason—and makes a fool of herself. Is that clear?"

"Yes," I squeaked.

"Okay," he said. "Get ready for class."

So *that* was it! I thought, falling away from his side like a doomed mountain climber. The dance was okay, but *I* wasn't! Inside, some important part of me dropped through black space, hit bottom, and died. I couldn't wait for class to be over. I wanted to go home and crawl into bed and shrivel up and die, too.

"Are you all right?" Jenny asked, as the bus approached her corner.

"Sure," I said, following her to the rear door and off.

"You've been so quiet."

"Well, yeah, I guess. I'm tired. We were up so late last night."

Jenny smiled. "Yeah. That was fun."

No sooner had the bus pulled away than Mom's car swerved into its spot at the curb.

"Hi, Mrs. Nordland," Jenny said, opening the door on the passenger's side for me. "See you Tuesday, Stephie."

"Okay. And thanks for having me over and helping me with the dance and all."

"My pleasure, madame." Jenny bowed and let me pass into the car.

"Hop in, Jenny," Mom told her. "We have to pick up Stephie's things at your house."

"Oh, that's right," Jenny said. She closed my door and scrambled into the backseat. "How are you, Mrs. Nordland?"

"Oh, just fine, dear. Have you two been enjoying yourselves?"

"We had a great time," Jenny assured her. "We choreographed a dance for the talent show last night and showed it to Mr. Oldham this morning. He said it was okay."

"Oh? Well. That's nice," Mom said, sounding less than pleased.

I glanced sideways at her, but she was concentrating on the road.

After we'd dropped off Jenny and picked up my duffle bag and record, we drove almost all the way home in a long, uncomfortable silence. As we turned into our block, Mom asked me the exact same question Jenny had: "Are you all right, Stephie?"

And I gave my same answer about being tired. It was far better than admitting the truth: Mr. Oldham had practically come right out and said I wasn't good. What else could he possibly have meant by that speech about practicing the dance and not making a fool of myself?

Mom put the car in the garage, and we climbed the stairs to the back door.

"Stephanie," she said, pausing with her hand on the knob.

"What, Mom?"

"I don't mean to be critical, but . . ."

I waited, the muscles at the back of my neck tightening. Mom never means to be critical. She just is.

"Couldn't you have at least tried to choreograph that dance yourself?"

"I did try. But Jenny's so much better at it. And anyway, what difference does it make? I'm the one who'll be *doing* it in the show."

"Well, that's my point exactly. If it's your talent, it should be your dance."

"Henry Porter's playing 'Für Elise' and he didn't write it. Beethoven did."

"Hmmmmm," Mom said, obviously not convinced. She gave an unhappy little shrug and opened the door. I lugged my stuff inside. Everything seemed three times heavier than before. Not just the duffle bag and all that, but my arms and legs, too. Even my head. Between Mom's disappointment in me and Mr. Oldham's concern about my making a public fool of myself, I was off to a great start. Stephanie Starr, ha! Stephanie Stupid was more like it.

I was dragging myself and my gear across the living room when Daddy suddenly burst through the front door. He was wearing what he calls his work clothes—baggy pants and a flannel shirt so old they don't have any real color anymore. He looks weird in them. Daddy seems more like Daddy in his *real* work clothes, a suit and tie.

"Hi, Stephie."

"Hi, Daddy."

"Anybody seen those little gizmos you tie leaf bags with?"

"They're in here," Mom called from the kitchen.

Daddy charged toward the kitchen, and I lurched up the stairs to my room.

"Lunch will be ready in a minute," Mom called after me.

"Okay."

It took me more than a minute to unload my stuff and put it away. Mom insists on things being put away immediately so they don't pile up. She's right, I suppose, but sometimes I think it would be so luxurious to leave it all in a slovenly heap smack in the middle of my room. Just for a little while.

When I finally started back down the stairs, I heard Mom and Daddy talking in the dining room. The first thing I noticed was that their voices sounded odd, kind of anxious and troubled about something. The second thing I noticed was what they were anxious and troubled about: me.

". . . I *love* Jenny," Mom was saying. "Who could *not* love Jenny? But if you ask me, Stephanie leans on her too much. She should have choreographed that dance herself, and I don't understand why she didn't."

"Maybe she's losing interest."

"Stephie? Never."

"It happens. One day a kid thinks he's going to be an astronaut; the next day, it's a fireman. And by the time he grows up, it's something completely different —a butcher, maybe, or a novelty gift salesman."

"It's not like that with Stephie, Sam," Mom insisted. "Dancing is everything to her. It always has been. Tell me one thing Stephanie likes better than dancing."

Daddy didn't have an answer for that. Because there *is* nothing I like better than dancing. Ballet, modern, jazz, rock 'n' roll, square dancing, folk dancing—whatever music there is in the world, I love to climb right inside it and *move* with it.

What was wrong with me, then? Why hadn't I tried harder to choreograph a dance for myself? Why did I go running straight to Jenny? Jenny certainly never came running to *me*.

8

I was up at five forty-eight the morning of the next talent show rehearsal, twelve minutes before my alarm was due to go off. It took me almost an hour to get dressed.

First, I thought I'd wear my red jazz leotard and tights and dance barefoot. I pulled the tights on, then stopped short. At dancing school we wear our leotards without underpants. But I suddenly felt shy about doing that at school. I took the tights off and put on underpants, then pulled the tights back on and inspected myself in my dressing table mirror. The underpants showed through in a truly stupid-looking line of lumps. I tried smoothing them down, but you could still see a thin line around the tops of my legs. I put the leotard on, hoping that would help, but the lumps grew even lumpier. So I stripped back down to my underwear and thought it over.

It was a jazz dance, which meant I could do it in jeans and sneakers. After all, practically everybody in *West Side Story* wore jeans and sneakers, except for the adults. I put on a long-sleeved blue plaid shirt and my newest jeans and the sneakers I'd bought just a week ago. Then I jigged around a little to test everything out. The shirt was all right, but the jeans were so stiff they practically cut me off at the waist every time I moved. I had to take the sneakers off to get out of the jeans. By that time I was shaking all over and had worked myself into a sweaty lather, so I stopped dressing and undressing for a minute, ran a wet washcloth all over myself, and reapplied my deodorant. Then it was back into the shirt, up with my old, tacky jeans, and on with the sneakers. Now I could dance, and without lumps. But what if Mrs. Deveraux decided the jeans looked too tacky? What if she was expecting a leotard?

I took off the sneakers, jeans, and shirt; yanked on tights and a leotard; then put the shirt, jeans, and sneakers on over that.

I was really too nervous to eat breakfast, but Mom gets upset if I don't, so I forced down some Rice Krispies and took off for school the minute she seemed satisfied that I'd eaten enough. You can always tell when that point arrives. She stops tapping her fingernails on her coffee cup and picks up the morning paper. She doesn't realize, of course, that she's tapping her cup and practically counting my mouthfuls, but she is.

This time the auditorium was packed with more than kids. There were trumpets and an accordion and a set of drums and parents toting all kinds of cases and music stands and whatnot. There were also a lot of kids who weren't in the show and a few teachers standing at the back with their arms folded and an "Oh, brother, where will it all lead?" expression on their faces.

I slipped into a seat next to Barbara, who was clutching the sheet music to "People." I knew this moment meant a lot to her. She once tried to drop the middle *a* in Barbara, like Streisand, but her parents made her put it back in. As I sat down she rolled her big brown eyes at me like a trapped and terrified colt.

"Are all these people going to watch?" she whispered.

"I hope not," I said, hugging my record to my chest so hard I nearly snapped it in two.

In a few minutes Mrs. Deveraux appeared onstage, waving her arms and calling for everyone's attention. Today she was decorated in various patterns of red. For a moment the buzz grew louder, probably from parents asking their kids what in the world that large, bright, peculiar creature was. Then there was a lot of shushing, like a steam radiator gone berserk, and the crowd finally settled down.

"I'm going to have to ask all parents, teachers, and students not directly involved in this rehearsal to please leave now," Mrs. Deveraux announced. People groaned, Barbara mumbled, "Thank God!" and I loosened my grip on my record album, but not much.

As soon as the extra people were gone, Mrs. Deveraux called us all down to the front of the auditorium.

She sat on the edge of the stage and held up a large white poster board.

"I have here a tentative order for our program," she explained. "I'm going to tape it to the edge of the stage right here, and I want you to find your name and be ready in the wings two acts before your own. Please stay out of the wings earlier than that, and go right out into the auditorium after you perform. Is that clear?"

We all nodded, a bit absentmindedly, because we were more concerned with locating our names on the list than with listening to directions. Mrs. Deveraux must have noticed because she whipped the list around so that only she could see it.

"The first three acts are Stephanie Nordland, Debbie Rosen, and Matt Greenspan. Will you three please go backstage? Stephanie, if you'll hand me your record, I'll tend to your music."

I was frozen numb from the shock of having to go first. I couldn't get my fingers unwrapped from the record album.

"Stephanie?" Mrs. Deveraux said. "Your music? Are you going to dance *to* that record or *with* it?"

I gulped and forced myself to hand over the album. I wasn't even warmed up! While Mrs. Deveraux messed around with the record player, I dashed backstage to do a few pliés and battements and stretches. Nervous chills kept sweeping over my body. I seriously wondered if I shouldn't plead illness—or maybe insanity—and go home.

But all of a sudden my music was playing, and there was nothing to do but dance. So I danced. At least I *think* I did. My body did *something* out there all by itself, without a bit of help from my brain. Did I smile? Did I even do the dance Jenny had choreographed? I wasn't sure. All I could see were the wooden stage and lights in my eyes and, occasionally, one of my own arms or legs swinging into my line of vision. It was very weird.

The best thing about my performance was that it ended. I ran to the edge of the stage and hopped off, only vaguely aware of a few hands clapping. I plopped down on the first seat I came to, out of breath and trembling, but glad it was over. Whatever Debbie Rosen did after me, I missed it.

When I finally calmed down enough to notice what was right before my eyes, Matt Greenspan was finishing up his flute solo, his cheeks puffing in and out like a squirrel working on an oversized nut. The next thing I knew, he had collapsed into the seat next to mine.

"Whew! Thank God, that's over," he muttered.

A warble of agreement trilled out of my mouth, which was still too numb to form words.

"You were terrific, Stephanie," Matt said.

"Me? Terrific? Oh, come on," I whispered, feeling my cheeks flush. For a few minutes nothing more was said. Matt tended to his flute. Onstage a seventh grader was attempting to saw a violin in half—or play "Spring Song"—whichever came first.

Then it was Barbara's turn. Mrs. Deveraux sat at

the piano and banged out her introductory chords. Barbara opened her mouth and began to move her lips. But nothing came out. Nothing that we could hear, that is. Her voice was too little to be heard over Mrs. Deveraux's pounding.

What I heard instead was Matt whispering to me again. We practically had to touch heads to hear each other. I couldn't help but notice that he smelled good, kind of soapy-clean with a little glow of perspiration from performing. Or was that little glow of perspiration *me*? I sank lower in my seat.

"You've been the best so far," he said. My ear tingled all the way to my shoulder blades.

"Oh, no," I told him. "I didn't even choreograph the dance myself. My friend Jenny did most of it."

"So what? I didn't write my music, either. And I didn't play it as well as you danced, that's for sure."

"Oh, come on," I said, so self-conscious I felt dizzy. To my great relief Barbara finished doing whatever it was she'd been doing, and we had to stop talking and applaud for her.

Soon she was sitting on the other side of me, fingers flicking over her chin. Matt immediately straightened up in his seat as if we hadn't just been talking head to head.

"Oh, I've never been so scared in my life," Barbara said. "I thought I was going to faint. Was I all right?"

Didn't she know? Couldn't she tell? Well, I guess sometimes you can't. "You were fine," I told her. What else could I say?

"Oh, I hope so," she whimpered. "I was so *scared*."

"I know," I told her. "So was I. So was Matt."

"You were? I couldn't tell."

"Scared stiff," I assured her. I turned toward Matt for confirmation, but he kept on staring straight ahead, as if he wouldn't dream of taking part in the conversation. You could tell he was thinking of a way to change seats without making it look too obviously a planned escape. You could just tell. And for some crazy reason, I didn't want him to. What I wanted, actually, was for Barbara to evaporate so Matt and I could do a little more whispering. Why that was suddenly so important to me, I really wasn't sure.

True, Matt is kind of good-looking, in a studious sort of way. And tall, taller than most of the boys and a lot taller than me. And he's so neat and clean, from the straight brown hair that falls across his forehead right down to his definitely *un*tacky jeans. But he was all those things in seventh grade, too, and I never even noticed.

Well, I was sure noticing now, but I didn't have the slightest idea of what to do next. So I joined him in staring at the stage as if Mrs. Deveraux might suddenly announce the cure for eighth-grade shyness instead of the next act.

But the acts went on and on, some good, some awful. Mrs. Deveraux smiled through it all, leading the applause and shouting, "Wonnnnn-der-ful!" and "Brrrrrrah-vo!" regularly. There were so many acts, we missed homeroom. But that was okay with me. I'd rather be in a show than in homeroom any day.

And I didn't get to sit next to Matt Greenspan in homeroom, either!

The minute Mrs. Deveraux dismissed us, Matt leaped to his feet. So did I, and we collided, my ear dealing a nasty blow to his elbow.

"Oh, hey, I'm sorry," Matt said while I pressed a hand to what was left of my ear and tried to keep my eyes from watering till he and the pain were gone.

"It's okay," I assured him. I figured I could still dance with one ear.

"You sure?"

"Yeah, really."

"Well, okay. See ya."

"See ya." I smiled bravely. He smiled, too, in relief, I think, that I wasn't going to haul him in for assault with a deadly elbow. Then he started up the aisle, his books in one hand and his flute case in the other. Watching him, I hardly even noticed the ringing in my ear.

"Who is he?" Barbara asked.

"Matt Greenspan," I said. "He's in Mr. White's homeroom, I think." But definitely *not* your typical eighth-grade boy!

Suddenly Mrs. Deveraux appeared beside me holding my record album and gushing my name. "Sssssteph-ah-nie!" she said, like a burst water main. "Your dance was ab-sol-*yute*-ly delightful!"

"Oh, well, I tried," I said with a shrug.

An odd, kind of wistful smile appeared on her face, and she just stood there, gazing into my eyes for a long time. Finally she broke her stare and noticed Barbara.

"Oh, Barbara, Barbara, Barbara," she said. Barbara perked up like a puppy expecting a table scrap. What could Mrs. Deveraux possibly think of to compliment her? I wondered. Mrs. Deveraux stared at her, too, for a minute, then said, "I think we can get you a microphone."

Show business can sure be rough!

I passed Matt in the hall four times that day, not counting the time we waved across the lunchroom. Funny how I'd hardly even noticed him before and suddenly we were bumping into each other everywhere. It certainly made changing classes more interesting. It even made being *in* class more interesting, because I could pass the time wondering if I'd see him again at the next change.

It's not that I don't like school. It's okay. But it's not like dancing school, where every part of me is alive and working, every inch from my brain to my big toe. In school I get by with about thirty-five percent of me awake and the rest of me daydreaming, miles and miles away. Until today most of the daydreams were about dancing: Nureyev and me taking curtain calls and being pelted with roses; Jenny and me hoofing across the stage in our first Broadway musical; me, defecting from Russia during a tour with the Bolshoi Ballet so I can be free to dance, dance, dance.

But daydreaming about Matt made for a nice

change of scene. I imagined how it felt to hold his hand. I pictured us laughing together over some private joke. And whispering, whispering, whispering. I could have kept it up all day, except Barbara stayed stuck to my side, fretting over whether or not she'd sung well. It got tiresome reassuring her every fifteen minutes.

I like Barbara more than any other girl in my class, especially because we can talk about show business. But show business to her often seems to mean just one thing: Barbra Streisand. Sometimes I think she really doesn't want to be a singer. What she *really* wants is to *be Barbra Streisand*.

Well, she's not Jenny, but she's a lot better than nothing. Anyway, there she was, glued right to me, when I arrived at my locker after last period and found Matt Greenspan waiting for me there.

"Hi," he said, smiling and brushing that cute lock of hair off his forehead. He was wearing his school jacket. He looks nice in green. It matches his eyes.

"Hi," I said back. So did Barbara. We all three stood there for a while, not knowing what to say next.

Matt took a deep breath and shifted his flute case from his right hand to his left. "Well," he said, "I—uh—your ear okay?"

"What?" I asked stupidly. I'd forgotten about our collision.

"Your *ear*. You can hear, can't you? I mean, I didn't . . ."

"Oh! My ear. It's fine."

"That's good."

"Yeah." I sighed. Matt bit his lip. Barbara's finger zeroed in on her worst pimple, just below her left nostril.

At this very moment, I thought, somewhere in the world, babies are being born. People are dying. War is being fought. And maybe someone is even discovering the cure for cancer. All that is happening like a whirlwind all around us, and here we are, the three of us, standing stiff and silent and stupid as a row of trashcans.

"Well, I guess I'll go," Matt announced at last.

"Oh," I said. "Okay."

Matt took another deep breath. Just as I was beginning to wonder if he had asthma or something, he said, "I really liked your dance this morning."

"Oh, no," I said, "I didn't do well at all. I was a nervous wreck."

"You didn't look it."

"Oh, gosh. Oh . . . uh . . . you don't have to say that."

"I know I don't have to," he insisted. "I wanted to, that's all. No big deal, you know?" His voice rose so high, kids passing us turned to gawk. I thought I'd die right there. They could bury me in my locker.

"Oh, for Pete's sake, Matt," I pleaded. "Quit it. You're embarrassing me." My voice burst out a lot louder than I had intended. I didn't mean to sound angry; I was just so embarrassed. But now a lot of kids had stopped to eavesdrop, and suddenly Matt was outblushing me by about three shades.

"Okay, okay," he said, backing away. "Sorry I mentioned it." And off he went.

"Hey, Matt, wait! I'm sorry—" I began, as he shouldered his way down the crowded hall.

"Hey, Matt, wait! She's *sorry!*" echoed a chorus of teasing, boyish voices, making things ten times worse.

And there was Barbara, her brown eyes bulging. She looked like a wounded duck.

"He was just saying all that stuff to be polite," I told her, my voice quivering. "He didn't really mean it."

"He didn't say it to *me*," she pointed out.

9

The next day was a walking nightmare. I passed Matt three times in the hall and twice in the lunchroom, and all he did was look straight through me with this hurt expression on his face. My heart stopped cold every time I saw him and then it raced until I thought it would explode right out of my chest. I couldn't think of what to say to him. I couldn't think at all. I felt awful.

Twenty-four hours ago my life was so uncomplicated, so simple and pleasant. All right, so maybe it did have a few rough spots: My mother expected perfection in everything I did; my father thought the most important thing in my life was a waste of time and money; my dancing teacher thought I was a fool, and my best friend was dancing circles around me. But other than that, things weren't too bad. I was getting along okay until Matt sat down beside me and started all that whispering. Boys, it seemed to me, were a lot harder than double pirouettes, especially when you didn't even know how to practice for them.

It didn't help much when Mrs. Deveraux stopped

me after music class and bubbled on about my dance all over again.

"You could be a professional dancer," she said.

"Well, I'd like to," I admitted, without much enthusiasm.

"Oh, that's wonderful, Steph-ah-nie!" Mrs. Deveraux said. "Then you must work verrrry hard and make your dream come true."

"Yes, I will."

"Don't let anything stop you, Steph-ah-nie."

"No, I won't."

"And you won't fail. I just feel it in my bones. If you want it, you can do it, Steph-ah-nie."

"Well, I'll try." Somewhere, deep in the pit of misery I was wallowing in, part of me took time out to wonder why Mrs. Deveraux was so concerned with my career all of a sudden. But I had problems of my own and really couldn't worry much about hers just then.

That evening I was practically jumping out of my skin by the time Mom got me to Jenny's house and Jenny said good-bye to all the Gianinos and walked with me to the bus stop.

"I've got to talk to you," I said when we were finally, *finally*, alone.

"I thought so," Jenny said. "You look like a baby kangaroo that can't make it back into the pouch. What's wrong?"

I fished around in my purse for bus money and in my head for the right words. Purse and head were about equal for messiness.

"There's this boy," I began, at last.

"Oh, yeah?"

The bus pulled up just then, and we had to pay and find seats before I could continue. But Jenny still looked extremely eager to hear more.

"His name is Matt Greenspan. He's in eighth grade, too. But he looks older. He's tall."

"Yeah? So?"

"Well, he's in the talent show, and after the first rehearsal he told me he liked my dance—*your* dance."

"You mean he liked the choreography?"

"Well, no, I guess not. I mean, not exactly." Jenny's eyes were twinkling, and I knew I was being teased. "He liked the way I *did* the dance," I admitted.

"Great! So what's wrong with that?"

"Nothing's wrong with *that*."

I looked out the window as the bus careened down Farmington Avenue.

"Steph?" Jenny called softly, her voice full of concern. "Come on. Tell me what happened."

"Well, after school he told me again how well I'd danced, and I told him to stop it because he was embarrassing me, and he got mad, and now he won't even say hello."

Jenny rolled her eyes. "Oh," she said, "I get it."

"You do?"

"To be perfectly honest with you, Stephie, you never could take a compliment."

"What do you mean?"

"I mean, if I tell you your hair looks nice, you say

it needs washing. If I say I like your new shirt, you say, 'Oh, wow, I don't know. I look awful in blue.' "

"But it's true," I protested.

"No, it's not. Your hair never looks dirty and you look perfectly fine in blue."

I tried to object, but Jenny didn't give me a chance. I got the distinct feeling that a skinny old lady across the aisle from us was trying to decide whether my hair was dirty and how I'd look in blue.

"Besides," Jenny went on, "when you put down a compliment, you make *me* feel like an idiot. It's as if *I* can't tell clean hair from dirty or a nice shirt from an ugly one."

"Oh," I said, as her point suddenly struck home. *That's* what I'd done to Matt. I'd made him feel like an idiot.

"It must have taken a lot of guts for Matt to compliment you the way he did. Couldn't you have just said thank you?"

"Well, you're supposed to be modest, aren't you?" I said. "I mean, you don't want me carrying on like Trisha Jones, do you, with one eye always glued to my reflection in the mirror?"

"There's a big difference between thank you and Trisha Jones," Jenny insisted. "It's one thing to hold private worship services for yourself and another to have a little self-confidence. Besides, thank you just means thank you for saying something nice. It doesn't mean you agree with what was said."

The little old lady's bright eyes followed us down

the aisle and off the back of the bus. I should have asked for her phone number so I could let her know how everything turned out.

"Okay, okay, but what do I do about Matt *now*?" I asked, as Jenny and I charged up the street, our dance bags slapping against our jeans.

"I don't know," Jenny said. "But it seems to me, if you hurt someone's feelings, you have to kind of build them up again. Especially boys. Boys get their feelings hurt very easily, particularly when they're trying to be nice to girls."

That must be why Jenny has so many boyfriends, I thought. She doesn't really date yet, but a lot of times when I go over to her house, there'll be three or four or five of them, all hanging around. The word is probably out all over West Hartford that a guy will never get his feelings hurt while being nice to Jenny Gianino.

"What's he going to do in the show?" Jenny asked, holding the studio door open for me.

"He plays the flute," I said, and skipped up the stairs ahead of her.

"Is he good?"

"I don't know. I was too nervous to listen. He *looks* like he'd be good, if you know what I mean."

Jenny nodded, her brow wrinkled in thought. We got to the dressing room and busied ourselves with zippers and buttons and such. Jenny paused with her belt half out of its loops.

"You know what I'd do?" she said.

"What?"

"I'd wait till the next rehearsal and after he performed, I'd compliment *him*."

"That's two weeks away."

"Then keep smiling and saying hello in the halls. But when the time comes, look him straight in the eye and tell him you think he did a great job."

"What if he doesn't do a great job?"

Jenny sighed. "Stephie, if you told a little white lie and made the guy feel good, would it change the course of history? Would it throw the earth off its orbit?"

"No," I admitted, but I couldn't help wondering how many people told little white lies when they complimented *me*? How did you know when someone was giving you a real compliment or when they were just being polite or trying to make you feel better? I was about to ask Jenny when Mr. Oldham's voice shook the walls.

"Ehh-vvv-ery-body out!"

An hour and a half later, soaked with sweat and throats parched, Jenny and I were stumbling off the floor when Mr. Oldham called us back.

"I want to talk to you two," he said.

I shivered, overheated as I was. My skin turned cold and clammy like a frog's. Oh, God, what now? I wondered.

Jenny and I followed him to his desk, where he sat down and put his feet up, leaving us to stand there, Jenny smiling and me trembling.

"I've got a couple of openings in my Workshop," he said. "I'd like you two to audition. Saturday, October 20, one o'clock. There'll be some competition, of course. Some new people coming in from other schools. You know what Workshop entails?"

Jenny and I both nodded, but he went on anyway.

"You're on call Monday through Thursday, eight to nine thirty. Saturday afternoons, one to four. You won't usually be called for every rehearsal, but you should be prepared to come every time you're needed. The only acceptable excuse for an absence is death— yours. You have to give up a lot for Workshop. You'll be doing your homework when other girls go on dates."

"We hardly date at all," Jenny said, laughing.

"Not yet, maybe," Mr. Oldham said, "but the time will come when you'll want to. You'll want to do a lot of things. But once you're in Workshop, I expect you to stay there. You get a lot of professional training free of charge. That means I invest a lot of time and effort in you. I expect you to do the same."

"Oh, we will," Jenny assured him.

I said nothing. There was a buzzing in my head and it was all I could do not to fall across Mr. Oldham's desk in a dead faint.

"Go home and talk it over with your parents," Mr. Oldham said. Not a smile from him, not the trace of a friendly glimmer in his eye. Somehow he'd managed to bestow an honor upon us and make me feel as if he'd banished us to Siberia for life.

Jenny was a bundle of giggles and hugs in the

dressing room. "The *Workshop!*" she cried, over and over, her voice squeaky with awe. "He asked us to audition for the *Workshop!*"

The other girls gathered around us, cooing and squealing with admiration and more than a little envy. I got hugged until I was breathless. How come everybody felt so happy, except *me?*

"The Workshop. I can't believe it," Jenny kept saying, all the way home.

I couldn't believe it, either. Why would Mr. Oldham ask *me* to join the Workshop? For one thing, I'm only thirteen and most of the others are much older. Anyone could see why he'd asked Jenny. She was so *good*. But why me?

An answer hit me just as the bus pulled into our stop and I saw the taillights of Mom's car. He'd asked me because he wanted Jenny and he figured she might not audition without me. It was a kind of little white lie.

"Mr. Oldham asked us to audition for Workshop!" Jenny cried the minute the car door opened. Even in the dark I could see Mom's eyes glowing like streetlamps.

"Really?"

"*Really*," Jenny assured her. "We have to audition with a lot of other people, of course. But he asked us. That's the important thing, isn't it? He asked us!"

"That's wonderful," Mom agreed. "Stephie, you must be so pleased."

"Uh-huh," I said, sinking deep into the backseat while the two of them babbled on. I was hoping

Jenny's enthusiasm would be enough for two, but very little gets past Mom. The minute Jenny was out of the car, she wanted to know what was troubling me.

"Nothing," I told her.

"He did ask you, too, didn't he?"

"Oh, yes, he asked me."

Mom brightened then and hurried home and into the house, eager to thrill Daddy with the good news. But one look at me in the light and she stopped short in her tracks.

"Something *is* wrong, isn't it, Stephanie?"

"What's wrong?" Daddy called from the living room. "What's wrong with whom?"

"Hi, Daddy," I said, grabbing the chance to escape from Mom and the revealing glare of the kitchen light. But Mom trailed me into the living room.

"Stephanie's been asked to audition for the Oldham Dance Workshop," she announced. She made it sound like an accusation, like "Stephanie's been beating up on small children."

Daddy flipped off the TV and looked from Mom to me, confused. "Is that good news or bad?" he asked.

"It's wonderful news," Mom exclaimed. "It's a great honor. Definitely a big step in the right direction."

Meanwhile, I opened my mouth, closed it, cleared my throat, and opened my mouth again. A tiny voice floated out and said, "I don't think I want to do it."

"What?" Mom cried.

"Why not, Steph?" Daddy wanted to know.

I shrugged. I didn't know exactly why not. I just knew I didn't want to go to that audition. Well, maybe I did know deep down inside, but I couldn't bring myself to think about it, let alone explain it. It was as if a switch in my brain clicked off every time I got close to the truth. All I could do was stand my ground and keep repeating, "I just don't want to, that's all. I just don't want to."

"Stephanie," Mom said, "you've been talking about the Workshop for years. You and Jenny have been dreaming about it for as long as you've been dancing. And now that you have the opportunity . . ." Mom stopped and sat down on the sofa, her hands folded neatly in her lap. "I don't understand," she said, eyes snapping in anger.

"Now, Ellie," Daddy told her, "Stephie must have her reasons. Don't you, Stephie?"

"I just . . . I don't know," I stammered. "It's a lot of work. Four nights a week and all day Saturday. And I've got the talent show, too. There'll be more rehearsals for that as it gets closer. I'll be up until after ten at night, and I'll have to be at school early in the morning."

"She's got a point, Ellie," Daddy said.

"Where there's a will, there's a way," Mom said between clenched teeth. But she didn't press the conversation any further. In fact, she barely spoke to me for the rest of the evening. Later, though, lying in bed, I heard her and Daddy talking in their room. They thought I was asleep, I guess. But I couldn't fall asleep. My head was too jumbled up.

"But she's only thirteen," I heard Daddy say. "The other girls are older. Even Jenny's older. What's the rush?"

"But why would Mr. Oldham ask her if he didn't think she was ready?"

"I don't know. But that's not the point. It's got to be Stephanie's decision. And apparently, with school and the talent show, she feels it would be too much for her."

"How can a dream come true be too much for her? It makes no sense at all. A chance like this. . . . If you ask me, she's being downright lazy."

"Stephanie *lazy*? She's always been a bundle of energy."

"Not lately, she hasn't. She's just not herself, and I don't understand it. How can she pass this up? How *can* she? It's ridiculous."

"Well, she *is* going through puberty, you know. Kids do get a little crazy at her age. It's not that unusual."

"Unusual or not, it could affect her entire life. Sam, if she wants to dance, she ought to *dance*."

"Oh, calm down, Ellie. The Workshop isn't a matter of life and death. Besides, it would be a burden on us, too, you know. We'd have to pick her up after rehearsals. I wouldn't want her waiting for the bus that late. All the stores are closed. The streets are deserted. Personally, I could do without all that driving back and forth. I do enough of it during the day. When I get home at night, I want to *relax*, by golly."

"Well, I certainly wouldn't mind doing it for her."

"That's very noble of you, Ellie. But she doesn't want to do it. Why is that so hard for you to accept?"

"I don't know. It just seems to me if you want something, you go for it. And you don't stop a minute till you get it."

"Look, you know my feelings on the subject. As far as I'm concerned, it wouldn't be the worst thing in the world if Stephanie didn't become a professional dancer. It's costing us a fortune and it's a very hard life and . . ."

I pressed my pillow over my head. I didn't want to hear any more.

10

Lazy. Maybe Mom was right. I was certainly beginning to *feel* lazy. Or worn out was more like it. I used to bounce out of bed every morning, ready for anything. Now everything from my arms to my eyelids felt like lead, and it was all I could do to drag myself out of bed and splash cold water on my face to get the circulation going.

That is, when I could manage even that much. The morning of the next talent show rehearsal, Mom had to wake me up. One minute I was sound asleep and the next she was shaking me by the shoulder and yelling, "Stephanie, you're late! Didn't you hear the alarm?"

I sat up and blinked at my alarm clock in confusion. Vaguely I remembered turning it off.

"I must have fallen back asleep," I said, rubbing my heavy-lidded eyes.

"Well, you've got twenty minutes to get to school. Get dressed; I've got breakfast waiting."

Mom pulled her red robe tighter around her waist and hurried out of the room.

I shook my head and yawned, trying to overcome the urge to curl up under my quilt for just a few more minutes. Twenty minutes till school, and Mom expected me to eat breakfast. Wasn't that just like her? I sighed and gingerly touched my toes to the cold floor.

Thirty-five minutes later, gasping for air and burping oatmeal, I dashed into the auditorium. There was a new poster hanging over the edge of the stage and a few kids were clustered around it. I didn't see Matt among them, but Barbara broke away from the bunch and met me halfway up the aisle.

"Deveraux has changed the order," she announced. "I'm fourth in the first half, right after you-know-who. You're last, just before intermission."

I collapsed into an aisle seat, too winded to ask who I-knew-who was.

"I overslept," I wheezed.

"I was wondering," Barbara said, flapping down a seat in the row behind me and resting her elbows on the back of the seat to my right. "I didn't think you'd drop out. A couple more kids have, though. Lost their nerve, I guess. Well, there goes 'Für Elise.' I better get backstage. Poor old Henry says he hates that piece. He's been playing it for six months. His teacher won't let him stop until he gets it all memorized."

"Break a leg, Barb," I said, with a weary wave as she skittered down the aisle.

"Thanks, Steph. You, too."

The way things are going, I thought, I probably will.

Peggy Moore did a tap dance after Henry's "Für Elise"—or his first two thirds of it, anyway. Somewhere in mid-arpeggio Henry stood up, knocking over the piano stool, let out a demented howl, and ran off into the wings.

"That's all right, Henry," Mrs. Deveraux called from the back of the auditorium. "I know you'll have it all memorized soon. Peggy? Take it away, dear."

During Peggy's dance Mrs. Deveraux kept encouraging her to look up, not at her feet, but every time she did, she forgot the next step. Some kids started laughing. It *was* kind of funny, but I felt too sorry for her to laugh.

After Peggy came Matt. So *that* was you-know-who! My heart which had already had a rough morning, banged louder and faster than Peggy's feet. He looked so sweet, so serious up there with his eyes slightly crossed in concentration.

This time I listened carefully. He *was* good. He played "Moon River," and the melody danced in the air like a butterfly, pure and bright and lovely. The same kids who had laughed at Peggy cheered when Matt finished. He grinned and made a funny little bow. Then he hopped off the stage and sat down in the front row—alone.

I remembered what Jenny had told me to do. I wanted to go over there and compliment him. But I couldn't move. I stared at the back of his head, at the way his hair fell just over his collar. I wished I could transfer my thoughts directly into his brain. I could almost hear them crackling across the auditorium like a CB radio.

Then something in Barbara's voice shattered my daydream like Annie Oakley's bullet blasting a clay pigeon. No, it wasn't her *voice*, exactly. They'd put up a microphone for her, and it had given out a great electronic scream like a wounded pterodactyl—or like Henry Porter during his five-thousandth attempt at "Für Elise."

The laughers in the audience grabbed their ears and hooted. What *creeps*!

Poor Barbara finished the song somehow, her voice tiny even with the mike. Then she slumped off the stage.

I couldn't go over to Matt now. I'd have enough to do comforting Barbara. And sure enough, that day and several others were filled with: "I can't do it, Stephie. They laughed."

"Oh, Barbara, they're idiots. Clods. You have a sweet voice." That was true. Small but sweet.

"Oh, yeah, sure, with a microphone. I can't . . ."

Around and around we went, passing through Math and English, lunch and gym, getting nowhere.

But that was later. As soon as Barbara's microphone was carried off, it was time for me to go backstage and warm up. And then it was time for me to dance. The thought of Matt sitting right there, front row center, while I danced made my bowl of oatmeal curdle in the pit of my stomach.

But after the first few steps, when my eyes accustomed themselves to the lights, I realized he was gone. It was all I could do to keep dancing. The lights blurred and bled together in front of my eyes.

"Take five, everybody," Mrs. Deveraux called when my music ended. "And *only* five. We don't want to run late. Good job, Steph-ah-nie."

"Thank you, Mrs. Deveraux." I could have reminded her that I'd tripped over my own feet on the third grand jeté and forgotten the steps to the next four bars of music, but I thought of Jenny and what she'd said about compliments, and didn't.

"Where *do* you study?" Mrs. Deveraux wanted to know, stopping me in the aisle. She was clutching my record as if holding on to me by proxy. I suddenly felt very uncomfortable. She seemed to want something from me and I couldn't figure out what.

"Oldham Dance Academy," I told her.

"Oh, you're getting *excellent* training, then," she said, staring at me until I had to look away. There was that strange sadness in her eyes. "You know, Steph-ah-nie, I envy you."

"You do?"

"Oh, yes. You are verrrry fortunate. You have talent and time. I had talent, too, once. Or at least I liked to think I did. But I ran out of time."

"You mean you wanted to be a dancer?"

Mrs. Deveraux laughed. "Oh, no, not a dancer. A singer and an actress, believe it or not."

"Oh, I believe it," I said. "I want to sing and act in

musical comedies on Broadway. But mostly, I want to dance."

Mrs. Deveraux stared at me some more, a really weird glow in her eyes. "I'm sure you will," she said, at last.

"Mrs. Deveraux, how come you became a teacher instead of an actress?"

Mrs. Deveraux smiled, but it was a lopsided smile, not a happy one at all. "It seemed to be the best decision at the time," she said. "It was more practical. It was safer, more secure. I told myself I'd get back to the theater. But somehow I never did."

Suddenly she brushed her hand across her forehead and turned toward the back of the auditorium.

"Everyone in the first act may as well go to homeroom," she announced. "Keep an eye on the callboard. We'll be rehearsing more often from now on."

Looking out across the rows of folded wooden seats, I saw Matt standing at the back of the auditorium. The minute Mrs. Deveraux finished speaking, he disappeared out the door. I'd lost my chance to talk to him.

11

"Stephie, you've got to be kidding!" Jenny screamed when I told her I couldn't audition for Workshop. I broke the news over the phone because I couldn't bear to be there in person to see her reaction.

"Why on earth not?" she wanted to know.

"A lot of reasons, Jen," I told her, my list ready from hours of rehearsing this conversation and working up the nerve to dial her number.

"Name one."

"The talent show. I'm really going to be busy with that and . . ."

"Mr. Oldham would let you off for that. You know he likes us to get performing experience."

"Sure, but between the talent show and Workshop, how am I supposed to keep up with my schoolwork?"

"For Pete's sake, Stephanie, how many more A's do you need?"

She had me there. And I was down to my last excuse.

"Jenny, you're two years older than me. The people in Workshop are even older than you—"

"So what?" she broke in. "Shirley Temple was a star when she was a *baby*. What's your stupid age got to do with it?"

"A lot," I said. "I'm not ready. I'm just not ready."

"How will you know when you *are* ready, Steph? Will a buzzer go off in your head? A gong? Dynamite?"

"I don't know. I just will."

"No, you won't. Nobody ever does. You just have to get out there and try and see what happens."

"No."

"Yes."

"No. I don't want to. I can't. And I won't."

"I don't believe it."

"Believe it, Jenny. *Believe it*."

There was a long, horrible silence on the other end of the line. I should have said good-bye and hung up. I'd made my point. What was I waiting for? Then, as the silence got even longer, it dawned on me that I wanted Jenny to say she wouldn't audition either, that she couldn't go on without me.

She said nothing of the sort. "All right, Steph," she sighed at last, her voice taking on a coolness I'd never heard before, "if that's the way you want it, that's the way it'll be, I guess. There's nothing more to say."

With that, *she* said good-bye and hung up.

I bet I can remember every time in the last seven years that I've had to go home from dancing school alone, without Jenny. There was the time she had chicken pox and missed two whole weeks of class.

And the week she went to New York City with her family to visit her cousin Michael before he went on tour in the show *A Chorus Line*. And there was the time she twisted her ankle so badly she had to keep her foot elevated for days and wasn't allowed to dance for three weeks. Eighteen times in seven years. That's it. Plus today, when Jenny stayed for Workshop auditions and I didn't. It felt so strange walking to the bus stop alone, as if I'd accidentally left something behind at dancing school. Part of my body maybe. It was scary.

For an October afternoon it sure looks like a November evening, I thought, watching Hartford swim by in a dismal gray mist outside my bus window. I wondered if Jenny was having fun at the audition without me. My stomach did a quick electric jig at the thought of the audition.

"I wish you were staying," Jenny had said, her face more pale than I'd ever seen it.

"I can't."

She didn't need me there. She was just being kind.

From across the studio Mr. Oldham's evil glare was upon me. It followed me, doubled by his mirror image, as I crossed the studio alone and descended the stairs. I'd waited until after class—the last possible moment—to confront him. I'd sidled up to him as the class filed into the dressing room and croaked out the toughest sentence of my life: "Mr. Oldham, I'm not auditioning for Workshop."

His response was to walk away as if he hadn't heard me. I was stunned. I'd planned to explain about how young I was and how I didn't feel quite ready yet. I'd wanted to ask if there would be another audition soon. But I never got the chance. His silence hurt more than a tirade would have. Apparently he didn't even care. The only effect my announcement had was to harden the expression on his face in kind of the same way Jenny's voice had cooled on hearing the news. It was as if they both had to pull away from me, as if I had some alien disease that might contaminate the pure atmosphere of their dancers' world.

I walked home from the bus stop through a light drizzle that chilled me to the bones right through my Windbreaker. By the time I let myself into the house, my hands were red and raw and my nose was dripping. Mom had left me a note on the dining room table: "Running errands. Back for dinner." That was fine with me. I was in no mood for conversation.

I peeled off my wet jacket and was massaging my hands with Mom's moisturizing lotion when I noticed that the letter lying next to Mom's note was addressed to *me*. The return address said "Music-Go-Round, Inc." and had a little striped merry-go-round above it with musical notes where the horses usually are. My heart leaped into my throat. I tore the envelope open with shaking hands, smearing it with lotion.

Dear Ms. Nordland,

Thank you for your letter of September 28. I'm sorry to be so long in responding, but at this time of year we maintain a rather sporadic schedule here at Music-Go-Round. As it happens, your letter came at a very good time. We will be casting a number of young girls this summer, particularly for our planned production of the musical comedy *Annie*, which, as you may know, is based on the comic strip "Little Orphan Annie®." The cast requires several "orphan girls." I am familiar with the Oldham Dance Academy and the excellent work of my friend, John Oldham, and so am sure you've had first-rate training. If you and your friend, Jennifer Gianino, can sing and act as well, I hope you will come to the regional open auditions, which will be held in Hartford around the first of April. Actually, I think it's easier to teach dancers how to sing and act than the other way around, so do let us have a look at you! A casting notice should appear in *Variety* sometime in March. Until then, keep studying and practicing.

> With best wishes,
>
> Tom Hitchman
> Music-Go-Round, Inc.

I read the letter through at least ten times, probably more. Each time I leaped into the air and squealed just like the first time. It was incredibly thrilling: a letter to me, a personal letter, from a famous producer. Well, maybe not *famous*, but definitely professional. And he was interested in us! He really was!

Or was he? I sat on the sofa and studied the letter

very carefully. Around April 1st, it said. April Fools' Day. Maybe the whole thing was a joke. Maybe Mr. Hitchman had never even seen my letter. Maybe his secretary had read it and decided to put me in my place with a joke answer. Or maybe his secretary had just thrown the letter away and the janitor had fished it out of the wastebasket and decided to have a little fun. Or maybe the whole office was in on it, sitting around laughing their heads off at the two stupid little kids who wanted to be in show business.

Stephanie Nordland, you're crazy, I told myself. This letter is *for real*.

Suddenly the day didn't look too bad, after all. I counted the minutes until I thought Jenny might be home from dancing school. I read the letter over a hundred or so more times, carrying it all over the house with me, even into the bathroom, as if it might evaporate if I let it go. I was in the kitchen, rereading it yet again, when Mom and Dad came home and the phone rang, all at once.

"I'll get it!" I yelled and whipped the receiver off its hook. "Hello?"

"Stephanie, I made it! I made it! *I made it!*"

Something a lot like a knife sliced through my stomach, leaving me breathless and weak. I gripped my letter and the receiver tightly while the pain receded.

"Oh, Jenny, I'm so happy for you," I gasped. "What was it like? Was it hard? Were you nervous? How many people auditioned?"

"Six, besides me. Yes, I was terrified. Yes, it was hard, really hard. It was like taking a class, only twice as long and six times more demanding. We were on toe for an hour and we had to do things we've never done in class. We had to do partnering and, Stephie, this boy I was paired off with couldn't lift me! I could hear him grunting and groaning and I didn't know whether to laugh, cry, or pray. But I made it! Me and two others. Oh, Stephie, I wish you'd been there. I never once stopped thinking about you and wishing you were there."

"Never mind about that," I said, focusing on the letter, forcing myself to ignore the ugly feeling inside me. "I've got news, too."

"You have?"

"Uh-huh. Remember when we wrote those letters?"

"Sure."

"Well, we got an answer."

"We did? Really? Who? What did they say?"

I barely had to look at the letter. I had it memorized. Jenny nearly blasted my ear off, whooping and hollering on the other end of the line.

"What a day!" she cried. "What a day! Hey, what day is it?"

"Saturday, October 20."

"Saturday, October 20," she echoed. "Remember that, Stephie. It's the happiest day of my life."

"Mine, too," I said, because I always say "Mine, too," or "Me, too," or "Me, neither," when Jenny makes a statement like that. It's kind of a habit. Only this time, Jenny had something really big to be excited about. She'd actually lived a dream-come-true. She'd auditioned for Workshop and made it.

All I had was a letter. And possibly another audition to face. Again my insides twinged painfully. What was it about that word—*audition*—that bothered me so?

12

First thing Monday morning I raced to my locker, hoping to find the social studies book I'd either lost or forgotten on Friday. Not only was I getting lazy, I was becoming absentminded, too. I wondered if a thirteen-year-old could be senile. But all that quickly took a backseat to Barbara.

"I'm quitting the talent show, Stephie," she announced.

She'd been waiting at my locker, her face almost as long and pale as the beige scarf hanging from her neck.

"You're kidding!" I said, steeling myself for another long day of keeping Barbara's spirits up no matter how mine were flagging. But she glumly shook her head to assure me she was not.

"Oh, Barbara, why? You were so excited about it." Where had I heard something like that before? Oh, yes. Mom talking about me and Workshop.

"I know," Barbara said, fiddling with the lock on the locker next to mine. She spun its dial this way and that and occasionally gave it an angry yank. "But

I'm quitting anyway. I've already told Mrs. Deveraux."

"Oh, Barbara! Why?"

"Because I'm no good. I'm a lousy singer."

"Barbara, you're not a lousy singer. You've got a sweet voice." Oh, God, I thought, here we go again. Poor Barbara!

"You don't have to say that, Stephie," she told me. "You've been very kind. Very encouraging. But you heard those kids laughing."

"But, Barbara, they're just a bunch of creeps."

"Maybe so. But in my case, they were right. Oh, I didn't want to admit it at first. I went home and I practiced for hours. I'll show them, I thought. But the more I practiced, the worse I got. My voice cracked. My throat got sore. Then I played my Barbra Streisand album and I played a tape of myself and . . ."

"And?"

"And I cried for an hour."

"Oh, Barbara."

We stood there for a few minutes, tinkering with locks while Barbara pulled herself together. I found my social studies book, but it didn't seem very important anymore.

Barbara twirled the dial in front of her faster and faster. "Maybe if I took lessons," she murmured.

"You mean you've never had lessons?"

"No. Never. Why? Did you think I had?" Her face brightened with hope.

"Well, I . . . ah . . . I certainly wondered about it.

Training is very important, Barbara. You ought to take lessons. All professional singers do."

"You're probably right."

"And then you could be in the talent show next year."

As if by magic, Barbara was suddenly all aglow again. "I'll make a comeback!" she cried, and gave a final yank to the lock. Much to our surprise, it opened. Barbara giggled and clicked it shut. "I need lessons," she said. "Why didn't I think of that before? Thanks, Stephie. You've really made me feel better."

"What did I do?" I asked. "You're the one who thought of singing lessons, not me."

But Barbara didn't hear what I'd said. She was too busy bubbling off into her own fantasy. "I don't know what I'd do without you, Steph. You're the best friend I've ever had," she said, then hummed a walking-to-homeroom theme for us, "You Don't Bring Me Flowers," a big Streisand and Neil Diamond hit. I tagged along, wincing with guilt at knowing I wasn't the best friend she thought I was. Or can you be someone's best friend when she's not yours? A sickly chill rippled through my veins. Was I to Jenny what Barbara was to me—half of a one-way best friendship?

At my seat in homeroom I tried to do my social studies assignment, but I couldn't concentrate. How could Barbara go from miserable to happy like that? I wondered. She might spend a fortune on singing lessons and still end up with nothing. What in the world was she so happy about?

Imagine that, I thought, imagine spending a fortune—and a lifetime—working for something, and then never getting it. A cold wave of terror washed across my body and I shuddered.

I stared at the questions on page 67 of my book: "Number One," I read. "At the time of the Revolution, each citizen of Connecticut was faced with an important decision: Should he or she remain a Loyalist or join the revolutionary movement? What might your decision have been? Defend your position."

I tried to picture myself in colonial garb, weighing the disciplined redcoats against the motley local crew. Instead I saw Barbara—or was it *me*?—ancient and wrinkled, tucked up in a bed, obviously dying. Whoever she was, there were tears streaming down her furrowed cheeks. Desperation gleamed in her eyes. "A lifetime wasted!" she kept saying. "An entire lifetime *wasted*." The light in her eyes dulled to a bitter, icy glimmer, and I found myself just about to burst into hopeless, frightened sobs when I realized where I was. The daydream faded, but a queasy feeling stayed with me.

What if that were me? What if I spent my entire life trying to become a dancer and I never made it? I'd grow old and ugly with bitterness and regret.

Was Mr. Oldham warning me that it could happen? Was that why he told me I'd make a fool of myself and why he criticized me so much in class? Especially lately. No kidding, it was really getting worse. Just the other night, he'd actually yelled at me, "Nordland, either wake up or get out. I've had it with you!" Jenny'd looked at me across the room with such pity, you'd think I'd developed a terminal illness. I was so embarrassed. I kind of wished I had.

The bell rang, and I yelped in surprise. I hadn't done my social studies. I'd run out of time. It was so easy to run out of time.

Maybe I should quit while I'm ahead—or at least not too far behind, I thought, making my way down the hall toward English class by habit. The queasy feeling left by my daydream still bore down on me.

"What?" Barbara asked.

"Huh?" I said. I hadn't even noticed that she was beside me.

"You mumbled something."

"I did?"

"Yes," Barbara insisted, laughing.

"Oh. I guess it wasn't important. Whatever it was, I've forgotten it now."

Boy, I was getting weirder by the minute. Now I was talking to myself out loud. I sleepwalked to my seat in English and went through all the usual motions of getting ready to take notes. Mr. Vanderbilt's bald head bobbed up and down as he took roll.

Immediately my mind was back on my dilemma. Maybe Daddy was right. Maybe dancing just wasn't worth all the time and effort you had to put into it. Maybe I ought to give it up. I could quit the talent show, too, like Barbara and the others. Why not?

Only how could I break it to Mrs. Deveraux? Or Mom? Or Mr. Oldham? What would Matt think of me—not that he thought much of me anyway. And what about Jenny? She'd taken all that time to choreograph my dance, and she was so excited about it.

I sighed and picked up my pen as Mr. Vanderbilt rose and went to the board.

13

As December 13th rolled closer, Mrs. Deveraux increased the talent show rehearsals to two and then three mornings a week. Getting up at six kept me bleary-eyed all day. I seemed to have no energy at all, or at most, no more than it took to stay up on my hind legs.

And rehearsals were lonely without Barbara. She may not be Jenny, and she may get on my nerves sometimes, but still, I missed her.

Most of the time I spent by myself, slumped low in an auditorium seat watching everybody else chat and chuckle and warm up and cool down. And, of course, I watched Matt. I still said "hi" to him in the halls and before each rehearsal, as Jenny had advised, but all he said back was "hi" in a tone one degree cooler than an ice rink. You'd think it would have cost him a month's allowance to smile.

The only thing keeping me going was the thought of performing Jenny's dance for her. I could already picture her flying backstage to congratulate me after the show, her eyes glistening and her smile lighting up the whole world. The very idea cheered me up.

I even knew what she'd say. First, to be polite, she'd hug me and tell me I'd been terrific, and then she'd ask me if the guy with the flute was Matt. And then she'd do *something*—this part was never clear—to make Matt and me friends again. I couldn't imagine what, but if anyone could do it, Jenny could.

It wasn't long, though, before even the hope of Jenny's support began to dim. The first Saturday in December, the Gianinos drove us into Hartford in their van. They planned to stay in town all day to do some Christmas shopping while Jenny was in class and then at Workshop. I'd have to take the bus home alone again.

Ever since the night of my announcement, the Gianinos avoided talking about Workshop in my presence. And since Workshop was very much on everybody's mind on the way into town, not much was said. To *me*, that is. But that was okay because Mr. Gianino had a lot to say to Ricky, who kept taking his seat belt off because it squeezed his tummy; and to Pete Jr., who kept telling Ricky all the different ways he could die without a seat belt.

"You could go right through that windshield, Ricky. And it'd shred your head. You'd be bleeding from a million cuts and—"

"Dad, make him stop!"

"Pete, quit it. But put your belt on, Ricky."

"It *squeee-eeezes* me!"

"You could fall on the floor and break your neck," Pete Jr. hissed. "Break it right off your—"

"Daaaaaad!"

Mrs. Gianino was busy with little Dawn, who was strapped firmly in her seat. Tiny as she was, she knew red lights when she saw them, and she saw a lot of them.

"Wed wight! Wed wight!" she'd squeal.

"That's right, sweetie. A red light. And now it's a *green* light, see?"

But Dawn was way ahead of her.

"Wed wight! Wed wight!" she'd say, pointing toward the next intersection.

Jenny looked at me and we both smiled. It must be nice, I thought, to have other kids in the house for your parents to fuss over. Mine just had me. I'd give a lot to hear them talking together in that hushed, worried way they have and find out they were concerned about some other kid for a change.

"Wed wight!" Dawn announced for the last time, and then Jenny and I were out in the cold, picking our way over the graying hills the snowplows had built.

"Oh, the new Workshop schedule is up." Jenny pointed out, stamping the last bit of snow off her boots at the top of the studio stairs. I followed her to the little cork bulletin board above Mr. Oldham's desk and read:

December 1–22: Soloists, Mon., Tues., Wed., 8:00–9:30, Sat., 1–3.
Corps de ballet, Thurs., 8:00–9:30, Sat., 1–3.

"Oh, good," Jenny said. "Just Thursday and Saturday. That works out perfectly for my finals before semester break."

I led the way into the dressing room. Suddenly Jenny screamed, "Oh, my God!"

I whirled around, expecting a ghost or an army of black widow spiders. "What is it? What's wrong?"

"*Thursday*. Thursday the *thirteenth*. That's your talent show, Steph."

"Oh! Yeah. Well . . . well, it's okay, Jen. You don't have to come. Really. I'll understand."

I couldn't believe I'd said that. Inside, I wanted to throw a temper tantrum, like a baby: "You have to come! You have to! You *promised*." But I didn't. I acted . . . well, the way Jenny would have acted, I bet, if things had been switched the other way around. It really surprised me.

"I do, too, have to come," Jenny cried. "I promised you I would. Besides, I *want* to come. I'll ask Mr. Oldham if I can miss one rehearsal. I haven't missed any yet. Of course, he did say . . ."

"The only excuse for missing a rehearsal is death. And he means it, Jenny. Listen, he might throw you right out of Workshop. It's not worth it. Really, it isn't."

"But I want to see you dance. More than anything else in the world . . . almost."

Almost. How could one little word hurt so much? Given the choice between me and Workshop, Jenny would choose Workshop. Not that I blamed her, but still . . .

"It's just like Mr. Oldham keeps warning us," Jenny went on, "about all the things we'll have to give up to be dancers. Dates and parties and fattening foods and stuff like that. It never used to mean much to us because we didn't have much to give up. But the older we get, the more there'll be, I guess."

"I guess so," I said.

Jenny blinked a few times and scrunched up her mouth thoughtfully. "But I'm not giving up yet," she said. "Let me think about it, okay? Maybe there's a way. There's *got* to be a way."

"Okay," I said. I turned around and unzipped my dance bag. I didn't want Jenny to see me cry. I didn't want her to know that her being at the talent show was the only thing I had left to look forward to. It was terrifying to need someone so much, someone who didn't need *me* much at all.

14

The next morning I knew something was wrong even before I opened my eyes. My head was pounding and the sunlight from the window burned my eyeballs straight through the lids. I swallowed painfully. Pulling myself up to a sitting position, I watched the room do fast chaîné turns around me for a few seconds, then fell back against my pillow and croaked, "Mom! Mom, I'm sick."

In no time at all, there was a thermometer in my mouth and Mom's hand clamped onto my forehead.

"I knew it," she was muttering. "I could see it coming. You, young lady, are going to see Dr. Terrell for a complete checkup first thing tomorrow."

"Ummmmm-mmmm-mmmmmmph," I said, around the thermometer.

"No ifs, ands, or buts about it," Mom answered, as if she'd understood me. "You've been tired day in and day out lately, which is not like you. You've been absentminded, which is also not like you. And you've been depressed, which is definitely not like you. And now you're sick. I don't care what your father says about adolescent mood swings and all that. Something's wrong and we're going to find out what it is."

"It's tonsillitis," I said, the minute she pulled out the thermometer. "That's all it is, tonsillitis. Dr. Terrell will say, 'Take aspirin for the pain, drink lots of liquids, and get plenty of rest.' You don't want to waste your hard-earned money on *that*, do you?"

"Yes," Mom said, her mouth a thin, determined line. "I do."

So she did. First thing Monday morning I was bundled into parka and boots and driven across town to Dr. Terrell's red-brick bungalow. Although I much preferred staying in bed, deep under my quilt where the world couldn't find me, and I wasn't at all sure I wanted to get well *ever*, I really didn't mind visiting Dr. Terrell. I like her a lot. She's friendly and cheerful and quick, all the things my old doctor was not. Mom switched me to a female pediatrician last year, partly because of her new feminist ideas and partly because Dr. Snyder, who I always thought basically hated kids, once wanted to take out my tonsils "just as a precaution."

"Unnecessary surgery!" Mom declared that night, pacing up and down in the living room.

"She does have tonsillitis at least twice a year," Daddy said. "Could you sit down, Ellie? You're making me seasick."

Mom perched on the arm of an easy chair. "Do you know how many unnecessary operations doctors perform every year?" she asked.

"A lot?" Daddy ventured, rubbing a spot over his

right eye as if Mom were giving him a migraine headache. "Too many, I bet."

Mom was up and pacing again. "*One* is too many! And yes, a lot—particularly on women."

Daddy sighed. "Ever since you joined that C-R group, you're a different person," he said.

"Yes, I am," Mom told him. "I am different. I'm better. And I'm taking Stephie to a female doctor."

"So how's your love life?" Dr. Terrell asked me after she'd given me the usual going-over.

I thought of Matt and answered, "Okay. Well, maybe not so hot. Well, actually, when you come right down to it, I don't have one."

"Hmmmmm," Dr. Terrell said, "plenty of time for that, I'm sure. How's the career going?"

"She doesn't have one of those, either," Mom butted in from her chair in a corner of the examining room. "She had a chance to audition for the Oldham Dance Workshop recently, and she turned it down."

Dr. Terrell whistled long and low between her front teeth. Her dark eyebrows did a little jig of surprise above the blue frames of her glasses. "How come?" she asked me.

"Heaven only knows," Mom answered.

You could see that Dr. Terrell understood that somehow Mom outnumbered the two of us. She changed the subject in a flash.

"Call tomorrow afternoon about the throat culture," she told Mom. "Till then, aspirin for the pain, lots of liquids, plenty of rest. Any questions?"

"Yes," I said, rasping over the pain in my throat. "Did you always want to be a doctor?"

"Yup," Dr. Terrell replied. "And from the time our family doctor laughed and told me little girls couldn't, I knew I *would*. I was the first woman to graduate from my medical school—which also happened to have been *his* medical school."

It hurt to laugh, but I laughed anyway.

Dr. Terrell winked at me from the doorway of the examining room. "Don't give up the good fight, Stephanie," she said.

The instant we were out of the building, Mom opened fire: "Did you hear what Dr. Terrell said?" she asked. "Even your doctor wants you to—"

"I don't care what my doctor wants," I said. "And you shouldn't have told her about Workshop. It's none of her business."

"I think it is. I think it has more than a little to do with your being sick."

"Oh, great," I said, angry tears welling in my eyes. "Now I have to prove I'm really sick. That's all I do, you know? Prove myself to everybody and anybody."

"What are you talking about?" Mom asked. What I'd said surprised me as much as it did her, but having said it, I couldn't seem to stop.

"I have to prove to Daddy that dancing is worth his precious time and money. I have to prove to you I'm Superwoman and can do whatever I set out to do faster than the speed of light. I have to prove to Jenny that I'm worthy of her friendship, that I'm just as bright and brave and wonderful as she is. I have to prove to Mr. Oldham that I'm one of the gifted, gutsy few. And now I have to prove to my doctor that I didn't intentionally infect my own tonsils."

"That's ridiculous," Mom began, but I didn't let her in. My aching throat was like a spur urging me on. I wasn't even sure I understood what I was saying, but I was going to get it said.

"It's not ridiculous," I insisted, while Mom angled the car toward home. "It's what I spend every waking minute doing, and I'm sick and tired of it. Please you, please Dad, please everybody. Well, I can't do it."

"Nobody ever said you had to . . ."

"Oh, yes, you did!" I cried. "You all do. You do it all the time. Just by being the way you are. I wish you'd all *just leave me alone!*"

The phone was ringing as I barged into the house ahead of Mom. For once I ignored it and headed straight for my room. As I climbed the stairs, I could tell from Mom's voice that it was Dad calling to check up on me.

"It's just tonsillitis," Mom assured him.

As far as I know, she never mentioned my outburst to him. But on the other hand, she quit harping about Workshop to me. For a while, anyway.

15

I missed four days of school, two talent show rehearsals, and two dancing lessons. When I arrived back in school at seven thirty on Friday, the auditorium was dark and, as far as I could tell, deserted. Confused, and feeling more out of the swing of things than ever, I started to close the door and leave. But a spotlight suddenly hit the stage, the curtains parted, and "Stayin' Alive" by the Bee Gees blared out over the speakers. Six seventh graders boogied onto the stage and did their disco number. The combination of music, lights, and dancing made my skin tingle. When the kids finished, I heard applause from the first row. A large figure stood up, unmistakably Mrs. Deveraux.

"Okay, keep it moving," she called. "Let's go. Let's go."

I hurried down the aisle and landed beside her just as she sat down again, and Matt and his flute stepped out in front of the curtain. I'd almost forgotten how cute he was. Lying in bed sick, I'd tried to conjure up his face, but it would never quite come in clearly.

It was so nice to look at him now, close-up and in full color, that I was surprised when Mrs. Deveraux hissed in my ear.

"Steph-ah-nie, you're late. I know you've been absent, but we're meeting at seven now. And we're running straight through the program, without stops, from now until show time next Thursday."

"Oh, I need to talk to you about that, Mrs. Deveraux. You see, my best friend, Jenny Gianino, called me and—"

"Shhhhh! Go backstage and warm up. We'll talk later."

When my turn came, I barely made it through the dance. My legs were so weak and wobbly from staying in bed, I felt like the scarecrow in *The Wizard of Oz*. I'd have to work doubly hard to get back in shape for the performance.

Intermission came after my dance, so Mrs. Deveraux gave everyone a five-minute break.

"Now, Steph-ah-nie, how are you, and what can I do for you?" she asked, draping an arm around my shoulder. A pudgy hand full of lavender nails dangled beneath my right eye.

"I'm okay, Mrs. Deveraux. But I have to ask you a very important favor. You see, my friend Jenny wants to come to the talent show, but she has Workshop rehearsal until nine thirty that night."

"Workshop? You mean the Oldham Dance Workshop?"

"Uh-huh."

"Your friend is in the Oldham Dance Workshop?

I'm verrrrry impressed. Maybe *you* will be in it one day, Steph-ah-nie. That would be something, would it not?"

"Yes, it would," I said, not about to go into the full story with her. "Anyway," I went on, "if Jenny's parents pick her up and drive her here immediately after rehearsal, she could see my dance—if you let me do it at the end of the second act instead of the first."

"Oh, I see. Well, it would have to be next to last. We do have the feeen-ahhhh-lee, you know."

The feeen-ahhhh-lee was when we all marched around the stage singing "There's No Business Like Show Business" and took our bows.

"I know," I said. "But it would mean so much to me if Jenny could see me dance."

"All right," Mrs. Deveraux said, "we can arrange that."

"Oh, thank you, thank you!" I cried, and gave her a big hug around the waist. She was very soft and pillowy all around. When I came up for air, I noticed Matt watching us from across the aisle. But the minute I looked back at him, he turned away, suddenly absorbed in some detail on his flute.

I spent the next week practicing every spare minute I had. I needed to build up the strength I'd lost while I had been sick, and I also wanted to know the dance backward, forward, sideways, and all the other ways Mr. Oldham had warned me about. When I watched TV, I sat on the floor and did stretches. I did my homework on the floor, too, with my legs in a split. If I boiled water for hot chocolate, I did pliés holding onto the sink. Waiting for the bathtub to fill, I did petits battements and ronds de jambe using the bathroom doorknob as a barre. And I spent so much time in the basement, Daddy said he was forgetting what I looked like.

Sometimes I could see progress. Other times I wasn't so sure. I couldn't stop thinking about that first lesson after summer vacation when I'd tried so hard to please Mr. Oldham and absolutely everything had gone wrong. An ugly little voice inside of me kept whispering that maybe I just wasn't any good at all. There were times I wanted to give up completely, but the thirteenth kept creeping closer and closer and in a state of near-terror, I kept on practicing.

And then the thirteenth arrived. Eight o'clock didn't creep up; it galloped. Both wings backstage were filled with people giggling and hugging and peeking through the curtain to count the audience. If it had been an Oldham Academy recital, they'd all be dead. Mr. Oldham always threatens to shoot anyone who acts unprofessionally backstage.

I claimed a quiet corner for myself and started my warm-up exercises. Every once in a while my heart would leap into my throat or sink down into my toes and tingle there. I forced myself to concentrate on barre work, using the wall as my barre. From across the stage came the trill of Matt's flute. That was one of the times my heart went haywire.

Suddenly it was eight fifteen, and Mrs. Deveraux sailed in among us, all silvery this time, right down to her boots. Even with her plentiful makeup, you could see that she was flushed with excitement.

"Qui-yet! Ab-so-lyute qui-yet now!" she hissed. "There is an ack-tyu-well audience out there, performers. Si-lencio, if you please."

Everyone settled down to anxious murmurs, occasionally pierced by a nervous squeal.

The first act seemed to take forever. I watched Matt from the wings. As far as I could tell, he didn't make a single mistake. He gave his funny little bow at the end, and the audience responded with a loud burst of applause. Somebody even whistled. Matt had to stay with the group on the other side of the stage, so once again I lost the chance to congratulate him right away.

The second act flew by. Before I knew what hit me, I was out there in the middle of the stage, staring at the blue folds of the closed curtain. My heartbeat was pulsing so loudly in my head, I wondered if I would even be able to hear the music. Then, as the curtain opened, I had my answer. There was my music, all right, and I was ready for it.

> Could be—
> Who knows?
> There's something due any day.
> I will know right away
> soon as it shows. . . .

From the very first step I felt terrific. Not only were my legs strong and sure, but *everything* felt just right, even my fingertips, my ears, and my smile. I was dancing all alone in front of a real, live audience and it felt wonderful. The beat echoed in my bones, and I couldn't make a mistake even if I tried. I wanted to go on dancing forever.

> The air is hummin',
> And something great is comin'.
> Who knows?
> It's only just out of reach,
> Down the block, on a beach.
> Maybe tonight . . .

The music ended too soon. I wanted to start all over again. But on came the rest of the cast, and soon I was singing "There's No Business Like Show Business" and really meaning it.

After the curtain closed for the last time everything happened exactly as I had imagined it. There was Jenny, the first one backstage, her black turtleneck leotard peeking out from under her green blouse. We hugged and hugged and she told me I was terrific and I told her she was terrific and we kind of laughed and cried all at once. Soon we were both hugging my parents and her parents. Even Pete Jr., Ricky, and little Dawn joined in the crush. And just as I knew she would, Jenny caught her breath from all the hugging and said, "Is that him? Is that Matt?"

I spun around, following her gaze. And there he was, right across the stage with his family, looking at me. I turned back to tell Jenny, but she was already beaming. In a glance I saw that he was smiling back. Then he looked from Jenny to me, and the smile stayed put. He must have guessed we were talking about him. He didn't seem to mind one bit. We might have all three stood there grinning like loons forever, but a little girl who must have been Matt's sister yanked at his arm and off he went. He did look back once, though, just as Henry Porter came tearing through the crowd shrieking, "I did it! I did it! I'll never have to play that stupid piece again!"

All in all it was a great night, the greatest of my life. I felt as if I'd climbed to the top of a mountain. I was giddy and breathless and the whole world was spread out at my feet.

16

All that backstage smiling between Jenny, Matt, and me sure didn't amount to much in the long run. The next day I made a huge special effort to go over to Matt during lunch and compliment him on his performance. He was sitting at a corner table with five other boys from his class. That meant I had to cross the entire cafeteria and say, "You played very well last night, Matt," while five heads paused over trays of macaroni and cheese to listen.

Matt said "thanks." He barely even looked at me. Instead he kind of slid his eyes sideways toward his classmates. Every one of them smirked. I felt like such a fool. I don't even know how I got back to my table, but if it were possible to blush yourself to death, I'd have been in mortal danger.

And for all my superhuman effort, when the new semester began after Christmas vacation, we went right back to our one-a-day "hi's" in the hall.

Jenny told me I'd probably embarrassed him again, and that I should have waited until his buddies weren't around. That was one of the few conversations we had time for as Jenny got more and more busy with Workshop. They had a performance scheduled in March and were really moving into high gear to get ready for it.

Meanwhile, I certainly didn't see much chance of ever being alone with Matt Greenspan. Every day my heart raced me to my locker, hoping to find him waiting there. The only person I ever found was Barbara. She'd completely gotten over not being in the talent show. Her parents had signed her up for singing lessons as a Christmas present and now she was *positive* we'd be in show business together. It was all she ever talked about. She even passed me this note right in the middle of Science Lab:

Dear Stephanie,

Someday we'll be walking down Broadway and a crowd of fans will rush up for our autographs and one of them will be You-Know-Who!

Yours in greasepaint,
Barbra

I could have wept right into my petri dish with its disgusting greenish-gray glob of bread mold. As far as I could see, both You-Know-Who and my career had been left behind on the mountaintop the night of the talent show.

I knew I'd hit bottom during Christmas break when my family and the Gianinos drove down to New York to see *A Chorus Line*. We'd been dying to see it for ages, but we never could get tickets. Then, out of the blue, Jenny's cousin Michael took over one of the roles in the Broadway company and six first-row-balcony tickets for a Saturday matinee turned up in Jenny's Christmas stocking.

Mrs. Gianino found a babysitter to stay with the little ones and the animals, and on the cold, clear Friday morning after Christmas the six of us piled into the Gianino van and barreled down Route 684 toward Manhattan.

For a while it was just like old times, all of us excited and laughing as we hustled our suitcases from the garage to the huge lobby of the Empire Hotel. While our parents got the room keys Jenny and I listened to the babble of foreign languages being spoken all around us and tried to figure out which of the other guests were with the Royal Danish Ballet appearing at Lincoln Center right across the street. It was easy to tell the ballerinas, with their hair pulled back into tight little buns and their brisk walks, toes pointed out and backs elegantly straight.

Later Mom and Daddy and I were unpacking when Jenny burst in to our room. She went straight to our window and pulled back the drapes.

"Stephie, come here," she said.

I joined her at the window and found that we were looking right down at Lincoln Center. Its modern white concert halls glowed in the cold winter sun and huge banners announced: THE ROYAL DANISH BALLET— TONIGHT!

"Someday, maybe," Jenny said in a hushed voice.

"Yeah," I breathed. "Someday. Maybe."

We spent the rest of the daylight hours walking all over New York. It was an unusually warm day for December, but we would have walked anyway. There were the Christmas window decorations along Fifth Avenue to see and the fashions in Bloomingdale's to admire and famous faces to search for in the mob around the theater district. And always and everywhere there were *people*, so many of them: bright, beautiful faces and worn, haggard faces, and every imaginable kind of size and shape and color and dress. Living in West Hartford, you could forget there were so many different kinds of people in the world.

"There are eight-million stories in this city," Mr. Gianino said in a deep, gruff voice, imitating the announcer on an old TV show.

"I want to be one of them," Jenny whispered.

"Me, too," I said.

Finally Saturday afternoon arrived and we were snaking through the crush of people outside the theater. We got settled into our balcony seats and suddenly, we were all very quiet. I, for one, just wanted to soak up the wonder of it: the expectant murmurs of the audience and the orchestra tuning up and the old-fashioned scrollwork and chandeliers around the theater. Then the lights slowly dimmed, and the conductor took his place in the orchestra pit. Jenny squeezed my hand and we grinned at each other in the darkness.

"Again! Step, kick, kick, leap, kick, touch, again!" barked a man's voice. I gasped in recognition. I could have sworn it was Mr. Oldham. But there were the dancers, moving so smoothly, so precisely, they seemed unreal, impossible, more like the spirit of wild horses than earthbound human bodies. A lump swelled in my throat.

As the dancers spoke and sang about their lives and what dancing meant to them, I thought they were all talking directly to me. Dancing, they said, made them feel special, beautiful, *alive*. And you could tell by the way their faces shone and their proud bodies strutted that they meant everything they were saying.

Great tidal waves of longing swept over me. I wanted to be up there on the stage with them. I knew exactly how they felt. I knew how, as each one stepped forward for a solo, he or she wished it would go on and on and on, forever.

The show reenacted an audition and at the end, the director chose some of the dancers and sent the others away. Tears burned in my eyes as the ones who weren't chosen slowly left the stage. The lucky ones stayed in line and looked ready to explode with joy. I found my heart following the losers. I knew how they felt.

The falling curtain was like a thief, snatching the brilliant, magical stage world away from me. I sighed with disappointment, then I was on my feet with everyone else, applauding until my hands burned. The dancers stepped out for their bows, smiling ear to ear as if it had all been more than worth the pain, the work, the disappointments. Of course it had been worth it for *them*; they were the winners. They'd made it to Broadway. But what about the ones who had reached out for that same dream with every bit of strength and hope and courage they had in them—and had come away with nothing?

We went backstage to see Michael, which was almost as exciting as the show itself. Close-up, you could smell the dancers' sweat. You could see the streaked greasepaint running into their eyes. They joked with each other and hugged each other and seemed to belong to a private club, no outsiders allowed. Even though we bumped into them in the cramped hallway connecting dressing rooms, there could have been a stone wall separating our world from theirs. Oh, how I wanted to leap over that wall! "I'm a dancer, too!" I wanted to cry.

Suddenly Michael appeared and swept Jenny off her feet in a bone-crunching hug.

"Oh, Michael, you were wonderful!" Jenny told him.

"Never mind me. I hear my baby cousin's in Workshop. How's Mr. Oldham? Nasty as ever?"

He kept his arm around Jenny's shoulders as he quickly greeted the rest of us. Then we stood back while the two of them compared notes about Workshop. Jenny looked so right standing there next to him, her cheeks flaming and her dark eyes bright. A chill shook me right down to my bones. Jenny had crossed over into that world. Without me.

17

"I don't understand it," Daddy said again, squinting through the darkness. Huge wet snowflakes swirled across the highway and pelted our windshield. The wipers whipped back and forth before my blurry eyes. It was a typical March blizzard, the kind that hits just when you're absolutely, positively sure spring is on its way. We were creeping home from UConn— the University of Connecticut—and I was sobbing.

"How can I ever face Jenny again?" I wailed.

"She'll forgive you," Mom said, patting my hand. Somehow the thought of Jenny forgiving me made me cry even harder.

"I don't understand it," Daddy muttered for about the hundredth time.

"Keep your eyes on the road," Mom warned him again. "We'll talk about it when we get home."

Farther and farther behind us at the university Jenny was being congratulated backstage after her first Workshop performance—perfect, of course— and I wasn't there. Not going backstage after a friend's performance is impolite, to say the least.

When it's a friend like Jenny who'd just about risked her life to be right where I needed her to be after the talent show, it's practically a sin. The crack between us that began when I didn't try out for Workshop was now a canyon.

When we were finally safe and warm in our living room, Daddy sat me down on the sofa, pulled up an easy chair to face me, and demanded, "Explain. Please."

"I don't know what happened exactly," I said. "The curtain closed and I burst into tears. I couldn't stop."

"That much I could see for myself," Daddy said. "But what was it all about? I mean, I know you've been moody lately, but that was incredible. You were high as a kite before the show and devastated after it."

It was hard to talk with my bottom lip quivering. Mom settled in beside me and took my hand. I held onto hers tightly.

"Stephanie," Mom said, "tell me the truth. Are you jealous of Jenny?"

"Jealous?" I squealed. "Of Jenny? Why would I be jealous of Jenny? She's my best friend."

"I know, but I meant because she's in Workshop and you're not."

"How could I be jealous of Jenny? *Jenny*, of all people! I'm happy for her. I'm *thrilled* for her. *She's* not the problem. *I* am. It's my fault. I'm so . . . so . . ."

A new rush of tears washed my voice away. Mom jumped up and got me another wad of tissues from the dispenser in the kitchen. I couldn't see to separate them, so I drenched them all at once.

"What is it?" Daddy pleaded. "*What* are you so . . . so?"

"I d-d-don't kn-know," I wailed.

"Stephanie," Mom said, softly, "Mr. Oldham did ask you to audition, too."

"But he's always hollering at me," I said. "One time he even told me if I didn't point my toes during a grand jeté, he'd cut my feet off."

Mom and Daddy exchanged a look, one I've always hated, that said, "She's so young, so naive, so cute."

"It's not funny," I cried. "He never yells at the other kids the way he does at me. He never yells at Jenny at all."

"Nobody yells at Jenny," Mom said. "Yelling at Jenny would be like yelling at a snowflake—or a buttercup. What would be the point? Jenny's a very unusual girl."

"I know," I said, "but if Jenny's a buttercup, what does that make me?"

Daddy turned red in the face trying to stifle a snicker. "A prickly pear?" he offered.

"It is not funny!" I yelled. "My whole career is over. I'm finished at thirteen. *It is not funny.*"

"Oh, good Lord," Daddy groaned. "Is dancing really worth all this? Is tripping around on your toes in little nightgowns—"

"Yes!" I screamed at the top of my lungs. "For once will you listen to me? *Yes! Yes! YES!*"

Daddy's grin gave way to a look of astonishment. "I guess it is," he said, at last.

"About time you noticed," Mom put in.

"It may be too late," I said, still shaking from my explosion. "Every time I go into that studio, Mr. Oldham treats me worse than the time before. This whole discussion may be for nothing."

"Is it or isn't it?" Mom wanted to know.

"Why don't you ask *him*?"

"Why don't *you*?"

"You mean go to him and tell him how I feel? Talk to him about all his insulting remarks?"

"Uh-huh."

"Mom, I can't. Daddy, tell her I can't. I'd be mortified. I'd be humiliated. Oh, I can't. Mom. Daddy. I can't!"

I was so upset, I got the hiccups. I ran into the kitchen for a drink and was trying to hold my breath and count backward from one hundred when the phone caught my eye. I should call Jenny, I thought. I should apologize for not going backstage. But I couldn't call her. I was too ashamed.

18

Early Saturday morning Mom and Daddy marched me up the stairs to the studio. A few girls were warming up at the barre, but their class hadn't begun yet. Mr. Oldham was on the phone. He hung up as we approached his desk.

"Mr. Oldham," Mom began, "we have a problem."

"Yes?"

"Stephanie seems to have lost confidence in her dancing. She's worried and upset and—well, she thinks you think she isn't any good."

Mr. Oldham pushed back his swivel chair and stood up. The glare from his eyes hurt my face like the sun when I woke up with a fever.

"Stephanie Nordland," he roared, "are you out of your mind?"

I gulped. Dancers stopped in mid-plié to stare at us.

"I asked you to audition for my Workshop. Why do you suppose I did that?"

"Be—cause you wanted Jenny?" I offered, without

much conviction, "and—and you knew we were best friends?"

Mr. Oldham slammed a fist down on his desk, and I practically jumped out of my skin.

"My Workshop is not the Humane Society," he bellowed. "I do not take in lost puppies and stray cats."

"Mr. Oldham," Daddy said, "maybe if we all calmed down and discussed this in a civilized manner?"

For the first time in the eight years I've known him, Mr. Oldham lowered his voice. "Of course," he said. "Why don't we step over here where we can have some privacy?"

He led us past the dressing rooms to a door at the end of the hallway. Inside was a cozy little room with a cheerful red rug, a gold easy chair, and a daybed covered with a granny-squared afghan and lots of pillows. Around the walls were shelves of books, mostly about dancing, and stacks of records. It kind of embarrassed me to be there, as if I were seeing Mr. Oldham in his underwear.

He sat in the easy chair, and the three of us settled ourselves among the pillows on the daybed.

"So you think you're no good, Nordland," he said. "Or you think *I* think you're no good. Then why do I waste my energy on you week after week? I've spent more time with you lately than with anyone else in your class. Have you noticed?"

I took a deep breath. Then, somewhere beyond terror, I found the strength to speak. "Yes," I said, "but it seems as if you spend most of the time yelling at me."

Mr. Oldham responded to that by yelling at me some more, this time loud enough to rattle my teeth.

"That's because you're driving me crazy! You're a very talented girl, Nordland, but it takes more than talent. It takes *guts*. What happened to yours? Something inside you died recently, and I don't understand why. Why didn't you audition for Workshop? *Why?*"

For once his yelling did some good. It shook me up so much, it dislodged the truth from under a pile of excuses so deep they'd hidden it even from me. But before I could speak, Mom tried to break in in my defense.

"Mr. Oldham," she said, "Stephanie's been under a lot of pressure. She feels she has to prove herself to everybody."

"That's not it, Mom," I said.

"But you told me . . ."

"I know. I thought that was it. But it's not. I wanted the pressure. In fact, most of it was coming from me, not you. I want to prove myself to you and Dad and Jenny and Mr. Oldham. It's exhausting sometimes, and I wish I could take a break from it, but I can't blame you for that. I set those goals myself."

"Wait a minute," Daddy said. "I heard a completely different story. You told me you just didn't feel ready yet."

I shook my head. "I guess I believed it when I said it, but it's not that either," I admitted. "Nobody ever feels ready. Jenny told me that, but I've always known it. I mean, would another year be enough? Five? Ten? Dancers don't have forever. I could run out of time."

"Then what is it?" Mr. Oldham said. "What *really* held you back?"

"I was afraid I wouldn't make it."

"So what?" Mr. Oldham said. "There's always another audition. If not for Workshop, for something else."

"But what if I *never* make it?" I whispered. "I couldn't bear that, Mr. Oldham. I watch other dancers perform and I want to be up there with them so much I feel like I'm on fire. But what if I never get to be a dancer?"

The spirit of the dying old woman hovered in the room, sickening me with her despair. "It seemed better not to try," I admitted weakly. "At least that way, I could go on pretending that maybe . . . someday . . ."

Mr. Oldham rolled his eyes heavenward as if I were more than he could handle alone and he needed God to send in the troops.

"Stephanie," he said, very quietly, calling me by my first name for the first time in years. "Do you *want* to dance?"

"Yes."

"Do you *love* to dance?"

"Yes."

"More than anything else in the whole world?"

"Yes."

"And do you dance just about every day, either here or at home?"

"Yes."

"Then you've already made it. Don't you see? You're already a success. *You are a dancer.* You are one of the lucky ones, Stephanie. You're one of the few people on earth blessed with the chance to do what you love best every single day of your life. No matter what the future holds, Workshop or Broadway or a dancing school of your own—or an accident that suddenly takes it all away—you can't fail because you've already won. Can you understand that?"

"I think so," I said. A new feeling of calm settled over me. I felt older, somehow, and a little less afraid of Mr. Oldham. "But Mr. Oldham?"

"Yes?"

"How come, when I showed you my dance for the talent show, you told me not to make a fool of myself? Did you think I would?"

Mr. Oldham smiled, not his usual nasty nervous-tic smile, but a real one, as a person instead of a dance master.

"I give that speech to all my dancers before their first solo performance," he said. "*My* teacher gave it to me years ago. It scared me into a hell of a fine debut! Besides, it's true. No student of mine ever goes on a stage—any stage, anywhere, for any reason—and makes a fool of herself."

So that's what he meant! I thought, remembering how I'd practiced my dance until I knew it backward, forward, sideways, and inside out. It *was* true: He'd scared me into a hell of a fine debut!

"You remember my other speech, Nordland?" Mr. Oldham went on. "The one about professionalism and the gifted, gutsy few?"

"You bet."

"Work on the gutsy part. You want a career, you've got to fight everybody for it—the competition, yourself, and your fears, and even me—if you dare."

With that, Mr. Oldham stood up, towering over the three of us on the daybed and looking ready to explode his way out of the tiny room.

"If that's all," he said, back to his normal bellow, "I've got a class to teach." And out the door he marched, with a nod to my parents so vague it seemed he'd already forgotten who they were and why they'd come. But I took a last look around that bright little room, knowing that no matter how much Mr. Oldham railed at me in the future, I'd seen another side of him there, the private, human side, and I didn't have to be afraid anymore. *That* side had called me a dancer.

19

Daddy and Mom went home and the nine o'clock class began, leaving me to sit alone in the dressing room with plenty of time to change my clothes and wonder what in the world I was going to say to Jenny when she arrived. Mom had phoned her house to let her know that we had to go in early. I was still too ashamed to talk to her.

I slumped on a bench, surrounded by mounds of jeans and jackets and dance bags gaping at me like gutted clams. The room was full of Jenny, of all those days in all those years when we'd huddled together here while I poured out the troubles of my heart for her to make right. Or when she'd spun dream webs about dancing that I'd gladly gotten caught in. Jenny filled up that room effortlessly. She filled *me* up, too. Without her, I'd be empty, limp, and lifeless, like those dance bags. Dancing and Jenny. Jenny and dancing.

And suddenly she was there. She hesitated in the doorway, her eyes like a surprised cat's, then came in, closing the door behind her.

"Hi," she whispered hoarsely, as if it were an effort to speak.

My heart sank. "Hi, Jenny," I said, choking up on her name.

She very carefully put her dance bag down on the bench opposite mine. Her back was toward me. She stayed like that, facing the wall of coats on pegs, for a long time. The room grew heavy with its own silence while from outside the door came the pounding of the piano and Mr. Oldham's insistent "*One*-two-three! *One*-two-three. *One*-two-three!"

"Ronds de jambe," I mumbled, just to be saying something. "That's what they're doing out there."

Jenny's head bobbed in agreement, but she didn't turn around. I felt paralyzed, hopelessly stuck to my bench. Then the music stopped, and I heard a little voice say, "Why weren't you there, Stephie? How could you not be there?"

Jenny was *crying*. I'd never, ever, seen Jenny cry.

The story burst out of me: how the sight of her onstage with the Workshop and so far away from *me* had overwhelmed me and how my parents had dragged me off, soggy with tears. Jenny finally sat down facing me, and we took turns sniffling.

"I waited and waited for you, Stephie," she said. "I couldn't believe you wouldn't come backstage. I'd *dreamed* of you being there to hug me and be happy with me. Didn't you know how important it was to me?"

I shook my head, while Jenny's image blurred and wriggled before me. I'd known it was wrong not to go backstage, and I was ashamed of myself for being such a blubbering creep, but I never realized . . .

Was it possible that Jenny needed me as much as I needed her?

"But I was a mess, Jenny." I tried to explain again.

"I'd rather have you there a mess than not at all. It was awful without you, Stephie. Even with other people there, I kept coming to the edge of this big *hole* where you should have been. I couldn't believe it. I just couldn't believe you weren't there."

Wiping away warm, stinging tears, I looked Jenny right in the eye. She wasn't just being polite. It wasn't a little white lie. It was true. Jenny *needed* me. Me!

"I'm sorry, Jen," I said. "I'm so sorry."

"I know."

"I'll never do it again. I promise."

"Okay."

All of a sudden I felt very shy, as if I'd just poured my heart out to a stranger. I guess Jenny felt the same way, because neither of us said anything for a while and we avoided each other's eyes. I wondered what it was that Jenny found about me to need. Who did she see when she looked at me? What was there for her to miss when it was gone? When I was little, I'd looked in my mirror and imagined Jenny. I'd have to start all over again. I'd have to get acquainted with me.

Chords from the piano suddenly crashed in on us. "One-two! One-two! Spot! Spot! Spot! Spot!" shouted Mr. Oldham.

"Chaîné turns," I said.

"Either that or he's calling his dog." Jenny giggled. I smiled, but I still had one more boulder to roll off my chest, one I'd lugged around a long time pretending it wasn't really there.

"I've been jealous of you, Jenny," I said. "Sometimes a little bit. Sometimes a lot. I've always wanted to be just like you, but I've been jealous of you, too. I've always thought you were perfect, you know? Never scared, never worried, never sad. Perfect."

Jenny licked her lips and took a long time answering. "Yeah, I know," she said, at last. "And if you want to know the rotten truth, I've kind of enjoyed having you look up to me. You know, around my family, it's hard to get noticed. Don't get me wrong, I love every one of them, but it's like a three-ring circus all the time. But with you . . ." Jenny paused, grinning shyly. "With you, getting noticed was something I could count on. You made me feel like a superstar—with a loyal fan club of one."

"Oh, I'm your fan, all right," I said. "But I don't think it can be exactly the way it was anymore."

"That's okay with me," Jenny agreed. "I really don't like trying to be perfect all the time."

"Me, neither," I said. Then it was my turn to giggle.

20

Regional open auditions for Music-Go-Round, Inc., were going to be held on Saturday, April 19, at—of all places—Mr. Oldham's studio. Mr. Oldham announced it himself one night after class and warned us to have a song prepared if we planned to audition.

"They'll be more interested in your dancing," he said, "but they'll be hoping you can also sing *loud* and *in tune*. And *smile*. That can make up for a lot of sour notes."

Jenny and I were smiling all right—excited, nervous, happy, anxious, impatient, and wildly hopeful smiles.

I asked Mrs. Deveraux to help me prepare a song.

"Ooooh, Steph-ah-nie!" she crowed. "How fahbulous! I'd be deeee-lighted!"

Mrs. Deveraux positively glowed, the pink flush on her cheeks clashing with her silky orange poncho as she swooped down the hall. Somehow the sight of her made me sad. It was my audition, my big chance, and she was acting as if it were hers.

"We'll work after school, or before, if that's easier," she said. "You'll be syuuuu-perb, Steph-ah-nie, I just know it! Oh, this is sooooo exciting!"

By the end of the day everybody, but *everybody* in the entire school knew I was auditioning for Music-Go-Round, Inc. If it had been up to me, I'd have kept it quiet until I'd either won or lost, but it was too late. Mrs. Deveraux told everyone.

At the end of the day, as I walked down the hall toward my locker with Barbara, people were still wishing me good luck: kids, teachers, even Mr. Hammerschmidt, the custodian. The audition was nearly a month away. Were they going to keep it up the whole time? Barbara was grinning and waving as if it were *her* audition, and I was so busy saying thank you to one and all, I completely forgot my ritual daydream about Matt waiting at my locker.

So, there he was!

"Hi, Stephanie," he said, kind of poised on the balls of his feet like a boxer ready to duck or run in case I did anything new to either humiliate him or physically damage him.

"Hi, Matt."

"I—uh—heard about the audition."

"Yeah. I guess everyone has. Mrs. Deveraux's very excited. She's helping me prepare a song."

"I know. She announced it in class. I guess she's been announcing it to all her classes. I'm surprised she didn't just use the intercom." Matt put his ever-ready basketball down between his foot and the lockers. Apparently he'd decided it was safe to linger awhile.

"It's kind of embarrassing," I said.

"Yeah, I guess so. Puts a lot of pressure on you."

We stood there for a minute, Matt and I and, as ever, Barbara. I fumbled with my lock a little. Matt cleared his throat and shifted his books from one arm to the other. Noisily yanking on my lock, I managed to turn toward Barbara and make a desperate face at her that Matt couldn't see. Finally she got the message.

"Hey, listen," she said, bumping shoulders and stubbing toes as she backed into the stream of passersby, "I've got to run. I've got a singing lesson in half an hour. Bye."

"See ya, Barb," I said. With great care I placed my books on the locker shelf and took out my parka.

"Hey, Greenspan, what's up?" a male voice called from the crowd. Immediately one of Matt's books slid off the pile in his hand and landed on my foot.

"Ow!" I yelped.

"Oops, sorry," Matt mumbled, stooping to retrieve his book. "Nothing much," he called back at whoever had caught him standing there with me. "Dropped my book here. How's it going, Miller?"

But Miller was already far down the hall making weird whooping sounds that may have been meant to embarrass Matt—or may have been his idea of normal conversation. You never can tell with an eighth-grade boy.

"Are you all right?" Matt asked.

"Oh, sure," I said, ignoring the rhythmic throb in my left big toe.

"Right on your foot," he moaned. "And you a dancer. God, how could I do that?"

"It was an accident."

"Yeah, but a really dumb one. Listen, I better walk you home, okay?"

"Oh, you don't have . . ." I began, but caught myself just in time. "Okay. Maybe you better."

While I got my parka zipped and my gloves on Matt took a deep breath and exhaled a tuneless whistle. "Well," he said at last, "which way do you go?"

I nodded toward the nearest door.

"Oh. I usually go that way," he said, indicating the opposite end of the hall.

"Oh," I said. As if I didn't know! I'd watched him go "that way" more times than I cared to remember.

We reached the door, me limping ever so slightly, and were in trouble already. Matt was juggling books, mittens, and the basketball. So I opened the door and held it for him.

"Oh, gosh, thanks," he said. "Are you sure your foot's not broken or anything?"

"Positive." I tried really hard for a charming smile, but my face felt like a blob of playdough. Now that I had him, what was I supposed to *do* with him? We were at the corner waiting for the light to change when Matt broke the silence.

"Remember that day in the hall when I kind of got

mad at you and ran away?" he said. "That was dumb. I'm sorry I did it."

"Oh, no," I said. "I'm the one who should apologize. I'm sorry I embarrassed you."

We crossed the street and walked on, taking turns taking the blame. By the time we reached my house, though, we'd decided to forget the whole thing and just start over. He couldn't come in because now he was twice as far from home as before and he had a flute lesson to get to. But he didn't rush off, either. He poked a pile of blackened snow with his boot tip a couple of times, checked the sky for more snow, and rubbed his nose.

"Hey, Stephanie?" he said, after a while.

"Yes?"

"You'll be great, you know. At the audition. I really think you will."

I took a deep breath. "Thank you, Matt," I said. "I appreciate your saying that."

Matt smiled. He was so cute, with his even white teeth, green eyes, and fuzzy brown earmuffs. "That is, if I haven't destroyed your foot," he added.

"Just one toe," I assured him. "I've got nine others. But thanks for walking me home."

"Any time. I'll see you around, okay?"

"Okay." I found myself smiling up at him with no trouble at all now. Although I was kind of wishing he'd offered more than "I'll see you around," it sure felt good to be friends again.

"I'll call you, okay?" Matt said, laughing.

"Okay," I agreed, smiling back now with no trouble at all.

Mrs. Deveraux brought me the sheet music to "Tomorrow," which was Little Orphan Annie's theme song in the show *Annie*.

"Not that I expect you to get the lead, first time out," she said, "but it never hurts to show them you're enthusiastic about the play they've chosen, right?"

I'd heard the song on the radio often enough that I already knew the melody. All I had to do was memorize the words, which wasn't hard. But singing under my breath around the house was a far cry from rehearsing with Mrs. Deveraux.

She drew the introduction out of the piano like a magician pulling an entire flock of pigeons out of thin air. The whole music room resounded with it.

"Deep breath and from the diaphragm," she urged.

Then my voice joined in. I had to sing my loudest to be heard over the accompaniment. "Loud and in tune." I could hear Mr. Oldham roar. "And *smile*."

For over three weeks I took deep breaths from the diaphragm, sang loud and in tune, and *smiled*.

On Friday afternoon the day before the audition, the words boomed out of my chest, pounding against the walls and the music. I raised my arms and waltzed around the room as I sang. The sun poured through the tall windows and flashed on my arms and in my eyes as I twirled up one aisle and down the next.

> Tomorrow, tomorrow,
> I love ya, tomorrow,
> you're only
> a day a-way!

I ended up on my knees beside Mrs. Deveraux, both of us holding the last note until I had to gasp for breath.

Laughing, she threw her arms around me and crushed me in a billowy blue hug. Then she took my face in her hands and looked me hard in the eye.

"Go for it, Steph-ah-nie," she said. "Give it your best shot. *All* those clichés. Hitch your wagon to a star. *Do it.*"

"I will," I told her.

She smiled and nodded, but her eyes glittered with tears.

Much to my surprise, I practically knocked Matt over on my way out the door.

"Hi, I've been waiting for you," he said. "I was wondering how long the audition would take tomorrow. When do you think you'll be home?"

"In fifteen minutes if I blow it. Not till dinner, maybe, if it goes well."

"I'll call you right after dinner, okay? I thought maybe we could—you know—celebrate. Go out for a Coke or something."

"Sure. That'd be great. Only—what if I don't make it?"

Matt held up both hands, palms facing me, eight

fingers crossed for luck. I crossed mine, too. Then for good measure he crossed his eyes.

I laughed, and decided I already had a lot to celebrate.

21

The audition was weird. It was weird right from the start, and it never improved. I mean, there we were, Jenny and I, going up those old familiar stairs, just as we do three times every week, only this time it was all different.

"I'm scared," Jenny breathed.

"Me, too."

Then she opened the door at the top of the stairs and we were sucked into a milling mob of total strangers. And when I say "strangers," I mean *strange*. These weren't kids gathering for a talent show. They were men and women, with hungry faces, determined to get a job or bust a muscle trying. Never in my life have I been so close to total panic, not even when squirming beneath one of Mr. Oldham's killing stares. In fact, I would have given anything just then to hear the old, reliable "Ehh-vvv-ery-body out!" But Mr. Oldham wasn't even there. His desk and the piano had been shoved to the front of the studio where a tall, gray-haired man began calling for our attention.

"Good afternoon," he said, when the nervous buzz

of the crowd had died down. "I'm Tom Hitchman. As some of you know, I'm the producer for Music-Go-Round."

Mr. Hitchman! I thought, and felt an insane urge to wave hello as if we actually knew each other. I quickly got control of myself, just in time to spot the insufferable Trisha Jones across the room, right next to the mirror, naturally. I nudged Jenny.

"I know, I know," she murmured. "The Weasel's here, too."

There he was, all right, his sallow face hanging above the piano like a polluted moon. Trisha. The Weasel. A studio full of lean and hungry strangers. Was I at an audition—or lost in a nightmare?

"I'd like to introduce our director, Sid Perkins," Mr. Hitchman continued. A chunky little man half-rose from his folding chair to a smattering of applause. He waved to one girl who winked back at him slyly. No fair, I thought. Little did I guess that "no fair" was going to be the rule of the day.

"And this is our choreographer, Adele Constanza," Mr. Hitchman announced, raising his voice and one arm as if presenting Miss America. I caught Jenny's eye as our mouths gaped in amazement. Adele Constanza was old and lumpy with crazy red wisps of hair sticking out all over her head. As if that wasn't bad enough, she was wearing holey tights, a repulsive purple leotard, and no bra.

"As I call your name, please line up in alphabetical order," she commanded. Everyone stood up and looked sharp.

Out of about a hundred dancers, half went home with nothing more than a curt "thank you" after the lineup. They never even got a chance to dance! Jenny and I—and Trisha—made it through the lineup; a series of leaps and turns single-file across the floor; a simple ballet combination; a jazz combination; some pointe work with partners; and a second, much harder jazz combination. All the while more and more people got sent home. Some left quietly; others shot the rest of us glances meant to destroy on contact; one got as far as the stairs and began to whimper like a puppy crushed by a truck. Ms. Constanza ignored them all.

Finally there were fewer than twenty of us left, and it was time to sing. Jenny did fine. So did Trisha, much to my annoyance. Then it was my turn, and all the nasty things I'd ever said about Wilbur the Weasel and his concrete fingers returned to haunt me.

He plunked out my introduction, sneering as usual, and I began to sing, giving it my all, just as Mrs. Deveraux had trained me to do, complete with a smile somewhere on my panic-stricken face. Unfortunately, though, Mrs. Deveraux had not trained Wilbur. He played so softly, I couldn't hear him—not if I kept belting it out the way I was supposed to. Loud and in tune, Mr. Oldham had warned us. From the diaphragm, Mrs. Deveraux had commanded. I did as I was told—and finished three measures ahead of Wilbur. Did he stop? Did he fake a final chord to save me? Oh, no, he *slowed down*. He milked those last three measures for all they were worth, while I stood there, stupidly short on words and long on music and mortification. If I hadn't been preoccupied with bracing myself for the inevitable "thank you," I would have leaped over the piano and bitten off his ugly blot of a nose.

But the "thank you" never came.

"Would you all just relax for a minute?" Mr. Hitchman suggested, then turned back to the desk to confer with Ms. Constanza and Mr. Perkins. I collapsed against the mirror next to Jenny, who patted my hand. "This is it," she whispered. All I could do was nod.

The Weasel began practicing a ragtime tune. Leave it to him, I thought, to be cheerful while the rest of us sweated years off our lives. Then Mr. Hitchman turned to speak to us, and the weirdest part of it all came to pass.

"I'd like the following people to report to New York for the final auditions in two weeks," he said. "Pick up a card with the address and time before you leave." As I held my breath and Jenny's hand he read the names of three boys and two girls we didn't know, then the girl who had winked at Mr. Perkins, the unbearable Trisha Jones—and *me*!

I was on my feet, shrieking with joy, thrilled straight out to the tips of my ears, before I realized he hadn't named Jenny. How could they not want Jenny? Surely there'd been a mistake. But when I looked at her, crumpled against the mirror, disbelief clouding her eyes, I knew it had to be true. Impossible, but true. Before we could speak, Ms. Constanza left the desk and came toward us. It *was* a mistake, I immediately thought. Of course it was. She's going to set it right now. But that wasn't what she had in mind. She knelt beside Jenny and put a gnarled finger on her arm.

"Listen," she said, "just for the record, I want you to know that we realize you're a remarkable young dancer. In a room full of remarkable young dancers, you're a standout."

"Then why . . ." I began.

She grimaced as if I were a bug annoying her, then refocused her attention on Jenny. "But you're not quite right for us," she explained. "I doubt you'll ever be quite right for musical comedy. It's not that you can't do the steps. Of course, you can. But there's a softness about you, a gentleness, a delicacy. . . . How do you feel about ballet?"

"I love ballet," Jenny said. "I dance with the Oldham Workshop."

Ms. Constanza nodded. "Oh, yes, they've gone to the top from the Workshop," she said. "The Joffrey. American Ballet Theatre. Stick with it, you hear? You've got a future; mark my words. A big future."

"Thank you," Jenny said, quietly, politely accepting the compliment in spite of how and when it was being given. I would have been bawling on the old hag's shoulder probably. But that's Jenny for you. And I still have a long way to go to catch up.

With a grunt Ms. Constanza stood and turned her piercing gaze on me. "And you," she said, "you dance like you have to keep the whole world spinning single-handed. Like one mistake from you and it's curtains for the planet Earth. Take it easy, huh? Not too easy, mind you. Just a little."

"I'm really happy for you, Steph," Jenny announced when we'd left the empty studio behind us and reached the street below.

"Thanks, Jenny. That was nice, what Ms. Constanza said to you, about your future and all."

"I know," Jenny whispered. Her voice sounded funny, kind of shivery, so I glanced over at her and saw her bite her trembling lower lip. Tears slid down her cheeks.

"Oh, Stephie, I'm so sorry," she said. "I don't want to spoil it for you, really I don't."

"That's okay," I told her. Me comforting Jenny? What an odd and amazing day it was! April 19, definitely a day to remember. "Believe me," I went on, "I know exactly how you feel."

Jenny sniffled and brushed her fingers over her cheeks. "Yeah, I guess you do. It hurts, doesn't it? It really hurts. Disappointment. Jealousy."

"Yup. Worse than blisters."

A shaky laugh broke through Jenny's tears, and I felt a surge of affection for her. It's one thing, I guess, to adore a perfect idol, an image in a mirror that you've really made up yourself, and quite another to love someone real.

They must have been frying up a fresh batch of potatoes at McDonald's. The smell practically made my knees buckle with yearning.

"I lost four pounds this week worrying about the audition," I said. "Well, it was four on Tuesday, but I gained back two."

"I lost three," Jenny admitted, smiling though her eyes were still moist and bright.

"Good enough." We whipped through McDonald's door, and each gathered a trayful of fries and a shake. When the first urgent gorging slowed to a civilized pace, Jenny stopped in mid-fry and said, "It's going to be like this from now on, isn't it? Sometimes I'll make it, sometimes you will, sometimes both of us, and sometimes neither."

"I guess so."

"We never used to think about that, did we? It never once occurred to me that we wouldn't live happily ever after, dancing side by side till the last spotlight faded away."

"Me, neither."

"We were younger then," she mused.

"Six months ago?"

Jenny laughed. "Well, it's been a long six months."

"Boy, hasn't it?"

We both slurped our milkshakes for a while. Visions of the past six months, from the talent show to New York City to UConn to the audition, danced through my head. The same scenes must have been doing their routine for Jenny because I looked up and caught her smiling.

"Feeling better?" I asked.

She nodded. "It was our first professional audition,

Steph, do you realize that? For better or worse, we were there. Scared silly, but there. I'll never forget a minute of it if I live to be a hundred and three."

"Me, neither," I said. And suddenly I was imagining Jenny as the old, bedridden woman who'd troubled me for so long. Except now the vision seemed different. It wasn't that she'd never suffered; she had, maybe even quite a bit. But she was at peace with herself, contented with her life in the long run.

"You know what, Jenny?" I said.

"What?"

"When I get to New York, the combinations will be harder, the competition will be stiffer and nastier, and the picking and choosing will be even less fair."

"Could be. So?"

"So they may throw me out on my derriere."

"Eat more fries. You'll have padding."

"No, *listen*," I said, laughing. "The point is, it won't matter."

"It won't?"

"Uh-uh. Well, it will, for a little while. But whatever happens, I'm still one of the lucky ones. I'm still me—and I'm still a dancer."

And Jenny said, "Me, too."

THE SARA SUMMER
Mary Downing Hahn

So far twelve has been a pretty rotten year for Emily. Nothing appears the way it was a summer ago. The kids at school call her Giraffe because she is so tall, and to make matters worse her friends now seem to spend all their time talking about boys and trying on make-up. Suddenly Emily feels an awkward outsider.

But things look brighter when Sara moves into the neighbourhood. Self-confident and assertive, Sara has an answer for everyone and everything. Not caring what anybody thinks of her, she disobeys her mother, smokes cigarettes, causes chaos at the class party and teases her little sister unmercifully. Emily is at first impressed by Sara's outrageous behaviour and even begins to act like her. But when Sara's tricks on her sister become too cruel, Emily knows she must stand up for the little girl, even at the risk of losing Sara's friendship.

A Dark Horn Blowing

DAHLOV IPCAR

Far out across the sands stretching silver-white into the darkening bay, the cow was calling. That mourning, that sadness; it filled my whole soul with its sorrow. But there were words crying in the sound, and it was not the cow that spoke those words, but a small man with a horn standing by a long, black boat there at the edge of the tide. The cow's lowing became the dark horn blowing, and then it was too late – if ever I could have turned back I could no longer.

'Here is a remarkable piece of fantasy; haunting title, magical opening chapter – I can promise you the rest won't disappoint.' *Naomi Lewis*

THE CHRONICLES OF NARNIA
C. S. Lewis

C. S. Lewis's wit and wisdom, his blend of excitement and adventure with fantasy, have made this magnificent series beloved of many generations of readers. The final book, *The Last Battle*, won the Carnegie Medal for 1956.

Each of the seven titles is a complete story in itself, but all take place in the magical land of Narnia. Guided by the noble Lion, Aslan, the children learn that evil and treachery can only be overcome by courage, loyalty and great sacrifice.

The titles, in suggested reading order, are as follows:

My Mate Shofiq
JAN NEEDLE

Since his best friend got himself killed playing chicken on the railway line, Bernard Kershaw has been at a loose end. He's got a gang, including a dead-smart girl called Maureen, but they don't do the sort of exciting things they used to.

His life at home's a mess as well, because his mum is ill in a way he doesn't like to think about. Although he still dreams about being a secret agent, or winning the war single-handed, things aren't really all that good.

Then one morning he sees the quiet Pakistani boy in his class turn into a violent fury to sort out a gang who are stoning some little 'curry kids'. Bernard gets involved, without meaning to at all, and finds himself up against the toughest bullies in the school.

He also finds himself in trouble of a different kind. For Shofiq's family, too, are in a bad way, and the grown-up people who are trying to help them appear to the boys to be set on breaking up everything.

Their attempts to stave off these disasters, and to make some sense of the things they see happening all around them, lead Bernard and Shofiq into confusion and violence.

'It's an angry and powerful novel – but much of it is very funny. The characterization is excellent; the dialogue is vivid. Thoroughly recommended.' *Reviewsheet*

When Marnie Was There

Joan G. Robinson

Brooding, lonely Anna, a foster-child, goes to stay with a kind Norfolk couple. There, like something in her memory, she finds the old house backing on to the creek. But it is the girl at the window who haunts her . . . Marnie, headstrong, often infuriating and somehow just as elusive when the two meet, as she had been at the window. Marnie becomes Anna's perfect friend, and though she finally vanishes for good, she has helped Anna to make real friends.

This is a thrilling, intense story, part mystery, part adventure, part fantasy, and will appeal particularly to girls of eleven and upwards.

Daredevils or Scaredycats
Chris Powling

'Thanks for saving my place, Mush. I'll have it now.'

Fatty Rosewell was a big bully, Every Saturday he used threats and fists to get himself one of the best places in the cinema queue. When Fatty picked on David Clifford, he was looking his most weed-like, all glasses and hair, but weedy David gave all the kids in the queue, not least Fatty Rosewell, a big surprise that morning.

Sometimes it's hard to know where cowardice ends and bravery begins. The most unlikely scaredycats can suddenly turn into heroes. In the course of their adventures, Teddy, Kit, Pete and Jimmy begin to find out just how many different kinds of courage there are.

'Entertaining and realistic, the stories take us into a world of dare and counter-dare, bluff and counter-bluff, catcall and playground scuffle.'

Recent Children's Fiction